Where
Love
Leaves
Us

The

Iowa

Short

Fiction

Award

Ψ

University of

Iowa Press

Iowa City

Renée
Manfredi

Where

Love

Leaves

Us

University of Iowa Press, Iowa City 52242

Library of Congress Cataloging-in-Publication Data

Manfredi, Renée, 1962–

Where love leaves us/Renée Manfredi.

p.   cm.—(The Iowa short fiction award)

ISBN 0-87745-444-2

1. Italian American families—Pennsylvania—Pittsburgh—

Fiction.   2. Fathers and daughters—Pennsylvania—

Pittsburgh—Fiction.   3. Italian Americans—Pennsylvania—

Pittsburgh—Fiction.   4. Pittsburgh (Pa.)—Fiction.

I. Title.   II. Series.

PS3563.A469W48   1994

813'.54—dc20   93-28456

                                                               CIP

98 97 96 95 94 C 5 4 3 2 1

For family, here and gone

Contents

ACKNOWLEDGMENTS

The stories in this collection previously appeared,
in a slightly different form, in the following
magazines: *Black Warrior Review,*
"The Projectionist" and "Truants"; *Iowa
Review,* "Bocci"; *Georgia Review,*
"Keeping the Beat"; *Michigan Quarterly
Review,* "Ice Music"; *Prairie Schooner,*
"The Mathematics of Pendulums"; and
Mississippi Review, "Where Love Leaves Us."
"Bocci" also appeared in *Pushcart Prize XVI.*
I wish to thank the National Endowment for the
Arts and the Research Foundation at Indiana
University.
Thanks also to Scott Russell Sanders, Tony
Ardizzone, Jack Heffron, and Lisa Dush.

*Where
Love
Leaves
Us*

The Projectionist

When I was fifteen I learned from my father the danger of love. I already knew about sadness, having watched him sink each year into what my mother termed his "Crazy April," a time each spring when he became quiet and distant and brought out in all of us the kind of caution one uses to navigate the pitch dark of a familiar room. My mother treated this mood of his with the same brisk efficiency that she did everything, made it seem no more mysterious than the bouts of asthma from which my father and I suffered: "Your father is having his April," she'd announce to my sisters and me as though his mood were a phenomenon of nature. I was twelve or thirteen before I realized that the world did not become strange and sad for everybody the way it did for us each spring.

My father had been married back in Sicily during the Second World War and his wife—Serafina, after whom I was named—was killed in April of 1945. The Germans had requisitioned the small fishing village near Palermo where my father's family had lived for three generations. After a year of relatively peaceful occupation, three young men tried to organize a resistance. They were considered war criminals and an arrest warrant was issued. They fled, went into hiding, and the men in the village were instructed to find them and bring them back by noon, dead or alive. Every quarter hour past that time, one person, chosen at random, would be executed. The women and children were ordered to gather in front of the courthouse. At twelve-fifteen the Germans executed an old woman. People panicked, were shot down as they ran. My father cautioned his wife not to move from beneath a fig tree no matter what happened. And that was where he found her when he returned, a bullet in her throat. She was eight and a half months pregnant and my father and the midwife delivered the baby, a girl, who lived for two days.

We were to say novenas for The Lady, as my mother called my father's first wife. If she hadn't died, my father wouldn't have come to America, wouldn't have married my mother, and my sisters and I wouldn't exist. My mother instilled in us the belief that The Lady was martyred for us and it was to her and a quirk of fate that we should be grateful for our lives.

Perhaps because my parents' marriage was arranged, it has taken me twenty years and two marriages of my own to understand that love should have something in common with happiness.

We lived in the Little Italy section of Pittsburgh, in one of the identical rowhouses on Kennett Square. The architecture recalled the typical photographs of the immigrants on the boat: crammed close together, listing slightly forward as though in eagerness or surprise. There was a certain timelessness to our neighborhood, the traditions and rituals born anew in each generation: women did laundry every day and hung it on lines strung from second-story windows while the grandmothers in heavy black dresses arranged their bulk on every porch stoop, buddhas of gossip and three o'clock espresso. In summer, the kids played kick-the-can and tether ball in the street. Doors were left unlocked. My father would not let us learn Italian, but the half-sung cadence of it drifting through our open windows is the earliest music I remember. My father was proud of his English, which he learned to speak flawlessly from John Wayne westerns, the King James Bible, and my mother.

I was fifteen in 1969, the year of drastic change in the city. The air was clearer, for one thing, as the filtering systems of the factories and mills improved. Developers began replacing the cobblestone and brick roads with asphalt. The local businesses and shops were slowly being overrun by modern supermarkets and department stores. Shopping malls were springing up in the suburbs and with them the cinemas that competed with the small, independent theaters like the Rialto, where my father was the projectionist. I began to understand, too, that we were poor—something I had never before considered—as non-Italians began moving onto our street; now we were linked to our neighbors through economic status and not by heritage.

My father took the changes in the city personally, grieved for the loss of the familiar. As I recall, his crazy April in 1969 began a few days after I had my first date. My mother never announced that his mood had arrived as she usually did every spring, and all these years I have been trying unsuccessfully to remember when he came out of it.

Carlo Benedetti was the son of the man who repaired our shoes. Not only was he one of the few from our high school to go to college, he was the first to drop out for what he deemed the uselessness of formal education. Carlo had recently returned to Pittsburgh and had quickly become the avatar of cool: he wore tie-dyed shirts, bell-bottom jeans, and a beaded headband to hold his shoulder-length hair off his face. He was the first boy my father agreed to let me go out with. Though he hadn't seen Carlo for years, my father approved of him chiefly because Carlo Benedetti, Sr., was president of the Pittsburgh chapter of the Italian Sons and Daughters of America, which was responsible for keeping Radio d'Italia on the public channel long after the audience for it had diminished. Besides, Mr. Benedetti had a talent for extending the lives of our ugly brown school shoes through the miracle of re-soling.

Carlo and I were going to see a movie at—where else—my father's theater. My mother and I argued about this all week: I didn't want my father present anywhere on my date, and I certainly didn't want to see *The Wizard of Oz*, which had been showing all month. The Rialto was losing money fast and it was dead last on the rotation list. My father showed "new" movies sometimes a year after they came out. Though he had secondary suppliers who provided him with films that were five, seven, years old, for one reason or another that month they hadn't sent him anything. As elected president of the local Moving Pictures Operators' Association, he wrote many letters to the managers of the shopping mall cinemas urging them to unionize and was incredulous when they went unanswered. "Fifteen years I have held this position, and it means nothing anymore?" I remember him saying.

Carlo was coming at eight, but I dressed early, anxious to put on silk stockings for the first time and the skirt my mother had shortened especially for tonight: at two inches above the knee it was our compromise between the thigh-high mini I wanted and what she considered the minimum length of modesty. The skirt depressed me a little: it was passably removed from the '50s, but had inches to go before it could move into the next decade. I knew, too, that Carlo had dated girls who were certain of their hemlines.

I completed the outfit with a tight, low-neck sweater, love beads and a headband from Woolworth's, bright red lipstick, and a generous spritz of my mother's Evening in Paris, which was hidden in the bottom of her drawer and was almost full.

I sauntered as casually as I could into the kitchen, where my father was sitting at the card table in the corner playing solitaire. My mother was at the stove preparing dinner, my sisters, Gemma and Frannie, at the table peeling vegetables.

"Wow!" Gemma said. "Are you going to a costume party?"

My father looked up from his cards and stared at me. Out of the corner of my eye I saw my mother's back stiffen, but she did not turn around. Watching him look at me I felt my defiance give way to foolishness and shame; the love beads seemed suddenly garish, the headband ridiculous.

My father shuffled the cards, glanced over at my sisters, who were looking from me to him expectantly. "Don't you girls have homework? That's the problem with you children. Everything is too easy for you. Education is a privilege, not your God-given right. Go." He waved dismissively at them. "Get busy with your schoolwork."

"I've done it already," Gemma said.

My father slammed his fist on the table. "Didn't you hear a word I said, young lady? Do you think you can get ahead in this world simply by doing what is assigned? If you have finished your work, you thank God that he has given you brains, and you work ahead."

Gemma turned and left the room. "You, too, little one," he said to Frannie.

"I'm five," she said, as though my father had never before considered this. "I don't have homework. I can't read."

"She's five," my father said to the air. "An American five-year-old. Mozart wrote a symphony at five. Michelangelo was painting at five. At five I was fishing professionally."

"All right now, Fella," my mother said. "Fella" was what she always called him, never Nicolo or Nicky.

He stared at me, the lacy web of veins standing out in his forehead. "I am a son of a bitch. I am trash. Take me out to the curb with the rest of the garbage. That's what you're saying to me with those clothes."

"This is fashion. Everybody is dressing like this," I said.

"It is in fashion to disrespect fathers? Fashion to go out in the world dressed like a *puttana*, fashion to throw the decency I have taught you back in my face? You will go out in public and shame me for a fashion?"

"Come now, Fella. The young girls are dressing this way now. You have seen them." My mother looked at me, then looked again, her eyes flashing with anger. "Who told you you could wear lipstick? Wipe that grease off your face." She threw me a dishrag.

"Yes, I have seen those young girls. Every time I see them I pity their fathers."

"This is a dress-up for a date. A date at which you will be present," my mother said.

"Don't you tell me about dates. I know about dates. I was young once. First it's a date, then he will teach her to dance, and before I know it I am a grandfather." He looked down at my legs. "Silk stockings. Since when do they make silk stockings for children?"

"Open your eyes, Fella," my mother said, a kind of warning edging her voice. "Open your eyes."

"Fifteen," he said dreamily. Then more harshly: "She's fifteen. In the old country girls still play with dolls at fifteen."

"The old country in your dreams, Sir. My mother was married at fifteen, my grandmother at thirteen."

Then my father did something that neither my mother nor I could have anticipated: he cried. Put his head in his hands and wept. I had never seen my father cry, not for funerals, not for joy, not for anything. From my mother's expression I saw that she probably hadn't either. She hesitated before going over and putting an awkward hand on his shoulder and did not dismiss me from the room.

He pulled away from her and stomped upstairs. A few minutes later we heard the creaking of the rocking chair overhead and the music of the tarantella that introduced Radio d'Italia.

"He'll come around," my mother said softly. "He's just surprised at how grown up you look."

Later, after his initial shock at seeing Carlo—"you did not tell me you were dating Jesus"—he was silent and remote. On the trolley ride home he seemed distracted and fearful. The date had not gone well. There were just five of us in the theater, including Carlo and me. Anytime Carlo reached for my hand, the aisle lights got a little brighter. When Carlo put his arm around the back of my chair, the house lights flashed on. "Christ," Carlo said. "Is your father always so subtle?"

I was furious with him, intended to say something on the ride home, but I saw the look on his face and I couldn't. I thought of the two-faced doll he'd bought for me once, each side of the head displaying a different expression. I used to turn it so that the seam that joined the faces was fronted, each one looking in precisely the opposite direction. This is what my father was like when he was on the cusp of his moody April, looking in two different directions from a kind of netherland, not able to be where and with whom he wanted, nor to be fully with us. There were times, for instance, where I saw on his face a kind of bewildered curiosity when he looked at us, as though we were only actors playing the roles of his wife and children and our performance was bitterly disappointing.

He spoke suddenly. "I wish to apologize for my outburst earlier. You could never shame me. You are my pride and joy."

A few minutes went by. "Anyway," I said. "Silk stockings aren't the greatest thing. They itch."

He chuckled. "Do you think Carlo enjoyed himself?"

"Yes, I think so," I said, my heart sinking a little. Carlo had been amused that my father was on our date with us, and teased me about watching *The Wizard of Oz*. I wanted to tell Carlo that my father didn't like the movie either, but I sensed they disliked it for different reasons.

"I hope this boy appreciates you. Did he tell you you were beautiful?"

I shook my head. "Carlo and I are just friends."

"That's the problem with young men today. They don't know how to appreciate a girl. That boy Carlo should give thanksgiving to God that you returned his interest. A beautiful girl, first in her class at school, a good Catholic from a respectable family. Just friends," he muttered. "He should be dancing in the streets."

The trolley stopped in front of Del Greco's Italian market, where we did all our shopping. The Del Grecos recently sold it for what was rumored to be a huge sum of money. It was to be torn down in a few weeks. Mr. and Mrs. Del Greco had owned the grocery and lived in the apartment above it for nearly forty years.

Mrs. Del Greco boarded the trolley, sat in the side seat across from us. We exchanged hellos.

"How have you been keeping, Ada?" my father said.

"I'm above ground, Nicky," she said. "I'm paying a little visit to my daughter, Selina. Her fourth baby, God love her. My son-in-law, the bum, won't keep a job. How much school does he need before he's smart enough?" Mrs. Del Greco didn't look well; she was thin, unkempt, and looked defeated and sad.

"The kids today need more schooling than we did," my father said. "What will you do, Ada, now that you and Sal have sold the market?"

Mrs. Del Greco stared ahead as though she hadn't heard. She leaned forward suddenly, touched my father's arm. Her eyes were bright and terrified. "God makes rules, Nicky, but he makes exceptions to those rules, do you believe?"

"Yes," my father said.

"I also," she said.

My father shook his head in sympathy when she got off. "It's good they are moving. The South Side is becoming unsafe. When I first came to Pittsburgh, South Side was almost all Italian. The women even washed the sidewalks in front of their houses, that's how clean it was. Look at it now. Mother of God. Crime, filth. Last week a group of punks broke into an old woman's house and beat her to death. A robbery. They got eight dollars." He turned from the window and stared silently ahead.

I had trouble sleeping that night. I heard my father get up and go downstairs, then the snap of cards being shuffled for solitaire.

Sometime later I awoke to the sounds of my father muttering and coughing in the hallway. My door was ajar, and I saw him crouch down beside the nightlight at the baseboard looking panicked and helpless. I walked out to him. "Do you need your asthma medicine?" His eyes looked strange—open but not seeing.

"I need fifteen minutes on a stopped watch." His voice had an eerie clarity and was more accented than the English I'd ever heard him speak.

"What do you mean?" I said, but then I understood that he was talking in his sleep, that he was moving around but he wasn't awake. "Okay," I whispered, afraid to disturb him. My grandmother always said that waking a sleepwalker could kill him or cause his soul to snap from his body and wander forever in the place where it journeyed in dreams.

My father walked in circles. "I can't find them, I can't find them anywhere. Help me. We have to find them." His hand on my arm was freezing cold. My heart was pounding. Just when I was about to go get my mother, he seemed to relax and I led him back to bed. In the morning, except for a lack of appetite, nothing about him seemed out of the ordinary.

Over the next few days the weather broke, the days were warm and lengthening, the nights coming on gradually with the cool deepening of twilight. My father and I sat outside for an hour or so before dinner each day, as was our custom each spring and summer. This year, though, I was also waiting for Carlo. After our first date, things got better; something in my father seemed to give way and he seemed resigned to the presence of this strange young man at our dinner table once or twice a week. He didn't say a word, either, about my appearance, about the skirts gradually inching up my legs, or the perfume and lipstick I wore when I was out of my mother's, but not his, sight.

"I have a little deal to make with you," he said to me one night as we were sitting outside. He'd brought out a bottle of wine and two glasses. "I want you to think about it before you say no. However, if the answer is yes, you may tell me immediately." He poured the wine. "The deal is, you forget about boys for one year, then I'll take you to Italy. You and I will take a little trip to the old country and find a husband for you." He pulled a sheet of paper from his pocket. "I have been calculating the expenses. If I put this much money aside every month, in exactly one year we will have enough for two plane fares, plus a little extra. But you must agree to stay away from these American boys. These boys who look like women with their long hair. They will come to nothing. You have never seen the old country, so you won't know what I mean when I say you can see God in the people there. All I ask from you in return is that you not date with boys here. Have some of that wine." He pushed the glass toward me and I took a sip. "Does it sound like a reasonable plan at least?"

I shook my head and kissed him on the cheek.

"Very well, then." He folded up and pocketed the paper officiously. "Good luck to you then, and may God have mercy on whatever mess you find yourself in." He stood.

"Wait," I said. "You've always said we were Americans, so why shouldn't I date American boys?"

He turned to me wearily, said, "You do not date boys, darling, you date hippies."

Carlo was there for dinner that night and he talked about his plans to hitchhike across the country next summer.

"What does that mean, 'hitchhike'?" my father said.

"You know," Carlo said, sticking out his thumb. "You stand on the side of the road and wait for someone to give you a ride."

"In other words, you are begging. Does your father know about this?"

"The old man and I don't talk much anymore," Carlo said.

"A smart boy like you," my father said. "Let me tell you, son, I remember how proud you made your parents. The days I went into the shop and your papa told me how you were so smart that they advanced you a grade. The scholarship to college. Now, suppose your papa gets sick, or your mother gets sick. They need you to help them and here you are, instead of earning money, you are begging across this great country."

"I have to live my life. There's more to life than earning money."
My father pushed the table back so hard that the wine spilled.

"Bedtime, girls," my mother said to Gemma and Frannie. She ushered them out of the room.

"What do you know of the value of money? What do you know of poverty? What do you know of not having enough money to get the hell out of a country where you forbid your wife to go to church for fear that it, also, will be under siege? Of not having enough to feed your babies?"

"I don't know," Carlo said. "But it isn't my fault that I don't."

"It is your duty to learn. People died to make your place here. We are Sicilians by birth, Americans by the grace of God."

"Well put," my mother said from the doorway. "He has a point there. Who would like some coffee?"

"I have one more thing to say. We are responsible for one another. Not just for members of our own family, but for all people."

"That's bull," Carlo said. "It's that kind of attitude that gets us involved in wars we have no business being involved in. We bully our way into countries and inflict our politics on them, all in the name of responsibility."

My father pounded his fist on the table. "I have seen your kind before. All you hippies who think you'll change the world with your peace signs and your long hair, you're nothing new. All talk, no action."

"I never said I wanted to change the world," Carlo said, but my father wasn't listening now.

"Three boys who wanted to be heroes. Stars in their eyes, a little wine in their veins. Three foolish boys who were directly responsible for the deaths of seventy-five women and children and the end of my happiness."

My mother carried the plates to the sink and stood with her back to us.

"My wife and baby died," he said to Carlo. "I delivered the child from her dead body. Small, but alive. They gave me sleeping powder and when I woke up two days later both my wife and daughter had been buried." He picked up his deck of cards and walked to the table in the corner. "This," he said, removing Carlo's fringed jacket from the bull horns on the wall. "This is not a coat rack." He threw the jacket toward Carlo. The bull horns were mounted on the wall in every house we lived in. They reminded my father of the horn of plenty, the cornucopia, and were a kind of silent prayer, a way to attract God's attention and providence without asking for it. The bull horns were high Sicilianism starry-eyed with the American dream: all good fortune, and living in the richest country in the world certainly counted, was to be treated as accidental if God was not to strike you dead.

My father shuffled the cards in the thick silence.

"Carlo, why don't you put on that nice music you brought over the other day?" my mother said from her station at the sink.

Carlo went to the record player in the corner and put on the Fifth Dimension.

My father looked up from his cards, tilted his head to listen to the music. "What is this song about fishtanks?"

"Excuse me?" Carlo said.

"Why are they singing about fishtanks? 'This is the dawning of the Age of Aquariums.'"

"Aquarius," Carlo said. "It's a sign of the zodiac."

My father stared at Carlo as though he hadn't seen him before. "You are a smart boy. Sometime I want you to explain to me how leap year works. Where do those years go?"

"They don't go anywhere. They don't exist," Carlo said.

"If they don't exist, why are they named? It must be that God saves those years for you. The last few years of a life are leap years. A second chance to make things right."

"It's only a matter of having an extra day every few years, Fella," my mother said.

"For every year that we live there are three that we don't. Or the other way around," my father said. "A whole lifetime of these invisible years. Where do they go?"

That night my father again walked in his sleep. This time he was standing in the hall, staring straight ahead and pantomiming the motion of pushing a child on a swing. He was murmuring in Italian. I watched him from the doorway. Though I couldn't understand Italian—and I now thought it was selfish of him never to teach us— I knew from the softness of his voice, the way certain words were caressed, that whatever it was he was dreaming, whoever he was pushing on that swing, was part of a happiness that none of us had anything to do with. Even his smile was something I'd never seen before: it began in his eyes, unlike his typical cautious amusement that merely flickered across his face.

I ignored my grandmother's superstition and whispered his name. He looked straight at me then turned, said up to the air, "Look, honey, your mother is here."

"It's only me," I said. The dim yellow light and the softness of his expression made him look at least ten years younger, as though he had hoarded his youth like pennies and was now spending it selfishly during the secret hours of the night. I called to him again and he turned. His eyes focused on me as he came a little more awake. "You're walking in your sleep," I said.

"I've been waiting for you."

"Why?" I couldn't tell now whether he was awake or asleep; he seemed halfway between the two. "I've been waiting. Pleasure and melons need the same season."

"Go back to bed, Daddy."

He sank to the floor, put his head in his hands. "All of my children are dead."

"No," I said. "No."

He looked up at me, glanced around. "How did I get here?"

"You were sleepwalking." I helped him to his feet, led him back to his bedroom.

"I must have made a wrong turn. I am facing the wrong way in the dark. Who will love me now?"

A few days later I came home from school and saw from the street that all the blinds in the house were pulled. My mother did this when one of us was ill, and at first I thought it was my sister Gemma, who had been sent home from school a lot in the past month. She'd become nervous, developed a skin rash, and had pulled out all of her eyelashes. The doctors found nothing physically wrong.

My mother was in the kitchen fixing a tray of cinnamon toast and orange slices. "Fella is sick," she whispered.

"Did you call a doctor?" I whispered back, but then I saw the crucifix and a bottle of olive oil on the counter beside my grandmother's old blue bowl that was used only for one purpose: a bad headache, a sudden or mysterious illness, even malaise, was said to be the result of the *mal'occhio*, or evil eye. My mother had always scoffed at these old world superstitions, called my grandmother—her own mother—a "sorceress with hot water." But her face was serious now. She arranged things on the tray and I noticed how bony her wrists were, how thin and worn-looking she'd become.

"What kind of sick is he?" I had never seen my mother perform the *mal'occhio* ritual before, not even in connection with my father's moody Aprils.

She hesitated. "I'm afraid we learned some bad news this morning." She handed me the *Pittsburgh Press* (which I have saved all these years). Headlined on the front page was: OWNERS OF ITAL. GROCERY KILL SELVES. Beneath it was the wedding picture of Mr. and Mrs. Del Greco. The article, quoting from their suicide note, said that they had planned this from the time they sold the grocery, that they wanted the money from the sale to go to their children: "We are old. We do not want that our children should have to take supervision of us. We do not want to pay all our lifely savings to an old people's home. We want to be buried by the Catholic church, being as we are sure God has forgiven us. Even God makes His exceptions."

"I need to ask you something, Serafina," my mother said, the tone of her voice making my heart ice over. "Have you noticed Fella doing or saying anything strange?"

"No." To this day I'm not sure why I lied. Except that deep down I suspected it was my fault. If I hadn't insisted on dating Carlo, we wouldn't have been on the trolley that night, wouldn't have seen Mrs. Del Greco, and my father wouldn't have been reminded that people like her were becoming obsolete.

"Because I'll tell you something," my mother said. "I have been through dozens of Aprils with him, but I've seen him like this only once. Years ago, this is, he tried to kidnap a baby." She paused. "Don't look at me like that. That mother was to blame. She allowed it to happen. This was before you were born and I was having trouble conceiving. They were relatives visiting from Italy. They stayed two months, and let me tell you, that woman never said a word when he took the baby to work with him every day. Held it all evening and fed it all its bottles. What did she think? Of course he is going to fall in love with it. He was depressed for months afterwards. It almost ended our marriage." She brushed past me with the tray. "Follow me. You need to have a part in this."

I followed.

My father was in bed and looked terrible. He was pale and unshaven, his eyes wide and bright with fever. "Did you hear about the old people?" he said. I nodded. "It's that bum son-in-law of theirs, that's whose fault it is. College-educated punk who wouldn't take the old people in. This would never happen in the old country. We took care of the grandparents. There was no such thing as homes for old people. That son-in-law should be taken before the law. He should be jailed for the rest of his life and the daughter shouldn't get a penny of the money. You," he said, pointing at me. "Don't you ever forget who you are and where you came from. If it is an American practice to put your parents out like the trash, I spit on America. I piss on this country."

My mother walked over to him, stroked his hair. She spoke in a soothing, comforting voice, as though to a child. He calmed a little then, looked up at her with a tenderness I'd rarely seen. She stood, took up the bowl of water and the oil.

"Isabella with the witch's brew," my father said. "I thought I would never see the day."

"All right, Nicolo," she said officiously. "Close your eyes." She turned to me. "How does this go?"

"You have to be on his right side."

She moved her chair.

I said, "Put three drops of oil in the water." She did so, and I watched as they separated, went to twelve, six, and two o'clock. "Say twelve Our Fathers, six Hail Marys, and two Apostles' Creeds." I dipped the crucifix in the bowl of oil and water and put it in my father's hand.

"Now what?" she said when she had finished the prayers.

"Now you petition your request to the appropriate saint."

"Who would be appropriate?" She looked down at my father.

I thought a minute. "Try Saint Christopher."

"What does he govern?"

"Protection for travelers."

She looked at me suspiciously then turned back to my father. "My request is that the dead rest in peace. That the souls in purgatory journey to heaven and not back to earth." She handed me the rosary beads from the bedside table. "Why don't you go say some novenas."

"For The Lady?"

She paused. "For us."

My father did not improve. Over the next two weeks he stopped eating and bathing. If I thought I didn't recognize him in his strange sleepwalking state, I certainly didn't recognize him now, this formerly fastidious man who once fired a concession stand clerk for dirty fingernails. He found a replacement to run the movies and stopped going to work. Stopped everything. He sat by the window all day, staring out into the street. My mother did everything she could to entice him back to us. Moved the kitchen table and radio into the living room. I stopped seeing Carlo, thinking that his presence would further aggravate my father. His sadness, my mother said, was closer to despair than to his typical April anguish, the difference being that in the former state there is too little hope, in the latter, too much.

"Come to table, Fella," she said one evening. "It's time for Radio d'Italia." She turned up the opening music of the tarantella but he quickly switched it off.

"No." He stood, said before he left the room, "There is no more Italy."

My mother stared after him. "What more can I do? What more can I do for your father?" She looked around at all of us. "Don't fall in love, girls. You give them your heart and they grind it like sausage."

"How many times have you been in love?" I asked.

"Too many. Too many times with the same man."

We were all aware now of my father's somnambulism, though something about it had changed: he often wandered into our room looking agitated or bewildered, as though the place he'd gone in dreams had disappeared or shut him out. A few times my sisters and I awoke to find both our parents in our bedroom, my father pushing against the window or the walls with the flat of his palm, muttering in Italian and saying over and over in English, "Help me." My mother would try to calm him down, then quiet my sisters, who did not recognize him in this state.

One night, my mother crushed a sleeping pill in a cup of chamomile tea for him hoping it would help his dreams be untroubled. We all went to bed early. The house and neighborhood were quiet and I fell instantly asleep.

When I opened my eyes, my father was sitting beside my bed, his hand around my ankle. The sky was still dark. I looked at him but didn't move. "Are you awake?" I whispered.

"Of course I'm awake."

"Well, I'm not always sure."

"I walk in my sleep sometimes, I know that."

"A lot," I said.

He ran his hand along my shin. "When did you start shaving your legs? Only American women do this, a custom I have never understood. It is like they want to be little girls again."

"How long have you been sitting there?"

"About a quarter of an hour. I was watching you sleep, trying to decide if it would be cruel of me to wake you."

I noticed then that he was wearing his coat and boots. "Where are you going?"

"I want you to come with me." He held out my jacket.

"Where to?"

"The movies."

I looked at the clock. "It's three in the morning."

"To you and me, but not to the people in the film."

"I'll come with you tomorrow."

"No tomorrows, darling, only right now."

"But I've seen *The Wizard of Oz* a hundred times."

"Tonight I want to show it to you the way I see it. It will be like the first time. Please. It's important to me."

I went in to tell my mother where we were going. "What's wrong?" she said, sitting straight up in bed.

"Nothing is wrong. He's fine, he just wants me to go to the theater with him. Go back to sleep. We'll be back in a couple of hours."

She lay back down. "My Evening in Paris is gone."

It took me a minute to understand she was talking about the perfume.

"I'll replace it."

"You and who else?" she said. "If there's any trouble, call me immediately."

I pulled my clothes on quickly and we walked to the Rialto, both of us wheezing with asthma when we arrived.

"Go in and have a seat," he said, unlocking the auditorium. "I'll make us a snack." He kept a loaf of bread in the booth with him; the projector got hot enough to make toast or warm egg sandwiches on. I used to call it magic toast: the same light that heated the bread lit the screen and illuminated lives larger than my own. I imagined I could taste the romance and glamour of the film, imagined it would become part of my body the way vitamins did.

My father started the movie and joined me in the balcony. "There she is, my Judy. Look how fresh and young. Break my heart."

We watched as Dorothy moved through the various indignities of Oz. My father was silent until the ending, when Dorothy was clicking her heels, ready to go home.

"And the ending is still wrong," he said.

"How do you mean?"

"They have it backwards. It's not Dorothy who dreams Oz, it's the wizard who dreams Kansas."

"I don't know about that," I said.

"Trust me. What is the Emerald City anyway? A place of cruel witches and frightening dwarves."

I remembered the first time I'd seen the movie. All the way through, I expected Dorothy not only to find the wizard, but to discover that he was her real father: why else would she be living with her aunt and uncle back in Kansas if not that her true parents were too magical for that black-and-white world? I remembered, too, how disillusioned I was to learn that the wizard was a pathetic, palsied old man behind a shabby curtain, how disappointed I was in her for dreaming of him in this way. Now, though, the ending seemed correct and inevitable.

"The sweetest face I've ever seen," my father said, looking at Dorothy as she shook off the dream of Oz and stared in bewilderment at the faces crowded around her. "I want to reach in and shake her. Warn her of the wolves like Minelli who turned her into a boozer and a doper, the bum. He gives Italians a bad name."

I turned to him, noticed for the first time that he was wearing the pajamas I'd bought him last Christmas as a joke: bright blue flannel printed garishly with characters from Flash Gordon. He had buttoned the top wrong and the tails hung unevenly. "Let me do this for you," I said, and corrected the buttoning.

The corners of his mouth turned up in a smile that did not reach his eyes. "You are beautiful. You are a beautiful young woman. What do I do with that?"

"What do you mean?"

"All the years I dreamed of having a family, I never saw myself as the father of a teenager."

"Did you think I would never grow up?"

"God likes to spring these brutal surprises on me. I wake up, my daughter is dead. I wake up, my little girl is a woman. I wake up, I no longer know where to shop for decent produce." He paused. "This boy, Carlo, does he love you?"

"No, I don't think so."

"Do you love him?"

"No."

"No, or No, not yet?"

I laughed.

"Promise me something."

I nodded.

"Promise me that if you lose your heart, you'll let your memory follow it. Otherwise, no one will know where to find you."

We sat in silence and stared at the white blank of the empty screen, waiting, it seemed, for something to begin.

Bocci

"Jesus Christ is a blood clot in my leg," Ellen says. "Right here in my calf, the size of a quarter." She puts her foot up on the bench where her mother, Nina, is sitting in front of the mirror applying makeup. "Do you want to see it?"

"Not now," Nina says, shadowing her eyelids with purple.

Ellen sighs loudly. She is ten, an ordinary little girl whose imagination sometimes intersects inconveniently with truth; all of her imaginary friends die tragic deaths and she grieves for them as though they were real.

Ellen sits on the floor beside Nina. Her mother is pretty today. She is wearing earrings and perfume, which she almost never does.

"Mama—"

"How many times do I have to ask you not to call me 'Mama'? It's infantile."

Ellen pauses. "Mother, my carnation didn't come today."

"It didn't? Maybe your father has finally had enough of spoiling you rotten."

Teresa of Ávila, "The Little Flower," is Ellen's favorite saint. Teresa levitated off the bed in her love of God and had visions like those Ellen herself has had: Michael the archangel has appeared to Ellen in dreams, called to her from the top of a white staircase. Until recently, Ellen would shake her head no when Michael held his arms open to her. But one night he sang so sweetly that she walked halfway up, he halfway down. Ellen sat in his white lap and he rocked her and looked at her with his great violet eyes that never blinked and told her that heaven was perfect but lonely. When he touched her, Ellen felt as though all the light in the world was inside of her, and when she awoke the next morning the sunlight seemed dim and she felt a heavy ache in her leg that beat like a heart.

Ellen's father, Sam, indulges her: every Saturday he has a white carnation delivered to the house for Ellen to wear as a corsage. All the nonsense about saints and angels is perfectly harmless, he said to Nina, and if a flower every week keeps her out of trouble and happy he'd gladly have them flown in from Brazil if necessary. "There are ten-year-old junkies," he reasoned to Nina. "There are ten-year-old children who hate their parents and run away and become prostitutes. Besides, it could be worse. She might be interested in Saint Francis and then she'd be asking for little peeps."

Ellen links her arm through Nina's. "Mother, last week in Sunday school Mrs. Del'Assandro said that when God is mad he puts out a contract on our lives. Jesus is the hit man. If a blood clot moves to your heart it can kill you."

"Mrs. Del'Assandro most certainly did not say that." Nina takes the bottle of perfume that Ellen is holding, says, "Clean your fingernails, Ellen, then go tell your father to come up and get dressed."

"Where are you going? Am I going?"

"No." Nina sprays a cotton ball with perfume and tucks it in her bra.

"Where are you going?"

"Just to the club for dinner and dancing."

"Then why can't I come?"

"No children tonight. Please go tell your father to come upstairs and get dressed."

Sometimes Ellen doesn't love her mother.

Ellen finds her father on the phone in his study. The room is cool, dark, though it is May and still afternoon. But her father is rich enough to have anything, even the night when he wants it and autumn air in spring. She sits on the desk in front of him, wraps the phone cord around her neck. "I am being hung in a public square! I am being persecuted for my belief in God!"

Sam swats her away, holds up a cautionary finger. She wanders about the room, picking up this and that, then shuts herself in the adjoining bathroom. She has been in here only a few times. The sunken tub is rimmed with candles. On the floor is a pile of tangled clothes. Some of Nina's makeup is scattered on the vanity. Ellen spritzes herself with perfume, dabs a little red on her lips. She lifts her long black hair off her neck the way she imagines a man might and pretends the shiver at the nape is from a kiss so soft it is like a quiet she can feel. Something is different inside her; this whole day she has been restless, has felt something that is part like hunger, part thirst, and part like waiting for Christmas. She turns from the mirror when she hears in the tone of Sam's voice that he is nearing the end of his phone call. One of Nina's bras is hanging on the back of the door. Ellen holds it up to her chest, stands on the edge of the tub so she can see this part of herself reflected. The cups are as puckered and wrinkled as Grandma Chiradelli's mouth. If she ever has breasts this big, Ellen thinks, she will have them cut off; otherwise she wouldn't be able to sleep on her stomach at night. She puts the bra on her head, hooks the shoulder straps over her ears, and fastens the hooks under her chin. This is how they look on Venus. All of the women on Venus have breasts on their head and are bald. All of the men are tall.

"Come out here, Elena," Sam calls to her now. She yanks the bra off her head and opens the door.

"How many times do I have to tell you not to come in here without knocking?"

"Mama sent me down to hurry you," Ellen says, and sits on his desk.

"Hurry me for what, pet?"

"Dinner and dancing at the club."

"Dancing? What dancing?"

She shrugs. "Mama says I can't go."

"Of course you can go. Are those your glad rags?" he says, looking down at her jeans and T-shirt.

She laughs. "I'll go and change."

"In a minute," Sam says. "Sit here with Papa for a while." He draws her onto his lap and she leans back against him.

"Papa, my carnation didn't come today."

"I know, angel. Papa is fighting with the florist."

Sam strokes her hair, says, "*Bella. Bella,* Elena."

"*Te amo,* Papa."

"How much?" Sam whispers. "How much do you love me?"

Ellen answers out of ritual: "To the moon and back and twice around the world."

"For how long?"

"Forever and a single day."

It is nearing dusk when they get to the club, a sprawling, white-columned structure that the Pittsburgh Italian Sons and Daughters of America bought from Allegheny township five years ago to use as a meeting place and family center. Sam, the vice-president of the ISDA since it was his money which imported the black-and-white marble and chandeliers from Sicily, named it the May Club in honor of the spring birthdays of his wife and daughter. It has the requisite swimming pools, upstairs banquet rooms, gymnasiums, and aerobics classes.

In the dining room, Sam, Nina, and Ellen are given their usual window table that overlooks the bocci courts. Ellen likes to watch the players. Already the men are in their summer suits and fedoras. Ellen knows little of the game except that the brightly colored balls have to come close to the small white ball without touching it, and that like church the players must wear suits and ties.

"Stop. Stop that," Nina says, and puts a hand on Ellen's leg to still its swinging. "What's this?" She touches a bulge in Ellen's knee sock. Ellen pulls out a stack of religious tracts that she has taken from church, pamphlets with such titles as "The Road to Salvation," and

"The Rewards of Piety." She carries them with her always and leaves them in restrooms wherever she happens to be. There are four ladies' rooms in the club. Ellen has spent a good part of every dinner here visiting each of them twice: once to leave the tracts, and a second to see how many had been taken. She is sure Saint Teresa would have done the same.

"Haven't I told you about taking these things?" Nina says.

She has brought too many tonight; usually she carries just enough to lie smooth inside her sock.

"Mrs. Del'Assandro told me I could have them. She says we should carry God wherever we go. Mrs. Del'Assandro says all God's angels would sleep next to me if they could."

"Mrs. Del'Assandro is a disturbed, unhappy woman." Nina holds out her hand for the tracts.

Ellen shakes her head, holds tight to them through her sock. "These keep the blood clot in one place."

"You make me tired, Ellen," Nina says.

"Everything makes you tired, Mama."

"Please," Sam says, "let's have a nice meal tonight. Everybody pleasant and polite. If anybody is tempted to speak unkind words, chew ice cubes instead."

Ellen stuffs her mouth with three and crunches loudly.

Nina turns to Ellen, her face red. "Go. Go amuse yourself then if I'm so unbearable."

Ellen begins her usual tour of the restaurant, sitting down with strangers who most of the time neither welcome nor acknowledge her. Only once or twice has anybody complained and so Sam indulges her in this, too. The times he'd restrained her ended with Ellen ruining her mother's appetite to get back at him. Ellen frightens him a little. No one else can make him feel as she does. He spanked her once and promised himself and Nina never again. Ellen was four, too young to remember. She had done some small thing and when his threats had no effect, he swatted her. But the harder he hit her the more resolute she became in her refusal to cry. He had felt something beyond fury; it was as though she were mocking the impotence of his rage. It had ended with Ellen locking herself in the bathroom and Nina coming home to find Sam screaming crazy, threatening things about what he was going to do to Ellen when she came out: Abandon her in a large, strange city where no one would ever find her. Nina had intervened and the next day Sam bought Ellen a pony. Thankfully, Ellen seems to remember nothing of this.

Ellen likes the darkness of the restaurant, the way the corners are so dim that unless she walks right up to the table the people are just shadows. She goes to the farthest corner where the aunts Anna, Lena, and Lucia usually are, the old, black-dressed women who do embroidery and talk of recipes and sorrow. And here they are tonight. Ellen sneaks up, crawls under their table and pretends she is Anne Frank, hiding from men who want to kill her. The veins in the old women's legs are maps for secret buried treasures. She sighs, draws her knees up. There is a nice breeze brushing across her cotton panties. All of the aunts wear the same thick black shoes with Catholic polish: shiny, but not glossy enough to reflect up when Sister Mary Margaret did a line check. Ellen knows which pair of shoes are Anna's: Anna always has her stockings rolled down around her ankles like sausages. Ellen loves Anna. After her papa and Grandma Chiradelli, she loves Anna best in the world. When Anna discovers Ellen under the table, her hands will reach for her, welcoming, as though it has been a thousand years since Anna last saw her, and she will fold Ellen against her and her skin and clothes will smell like rubbing alcohol and lavender and grass. Anna is the only one who doesn't laugh or roll her eyes when Ellen discloses her dreams of angels, and it is to Anna alone that Ellen has confessed her desire of becoming a nun or a saint.

There is dancing going on upstairs; Ellen hears the music of a tarantella, the stomping of feet.

"Wedding," one of the aunts says. "Sal Benedetti and Rosa, the last of Vito's daughters, God bless her." The other two murmur agreement and Ellen hears them put their forks down in order to cross themselves.

"Which one is Rosa?" Lucia says.

"The ugly one," Lena, the mean aunt, says. She once told Ellen she would go to hell for wearing so much jewelry and that in hell her necklaces and bracelets would turn into snakes.

"Lena, so what ugly? What's the difference when the lights are out?" Lucia says. "Rosa is a work of God but not his masterpiece."

"I had the most beautiful gown for my wedding night," Anna says.

"I also," Lena says. "The chair looked very nice in it. All that needlework my mother did on it, and for what? They all want you naked."

The aunts chuckle.

Ellen searches through her stack of pamphlets until she comes to the one with "La Pietà" on the front. She folds it into a tiny square and slips it beneath Anna's shoelaces. Anna will find it there later when she is undressing and say a prayer for her dead and for Ellen.

"I feel a little mouse at my feet," Anna says, and lifts the edge of the tablecloth to look at Ellen. Lena and Lucia peer down after her.

"Buena sera, Anna."

"Look at the way she lies," Lena says. "Puttana. Good girls don't lie in public with their legs spread like crickets."

"I'm not a good girl. I'm spirited and tiring."

"Si, spirito, e un valle di lacrime," Lena says.

"No speaka, no capische," Ellen says, and covers her ears, but she gets it anyway. Spirited and tearful. A valley of tears.

"Hopeless," Lena says, and continues eating.

"And how is the future little novitiate?" Anna says, and hugs Ellen tight against her. "My, but it's good to see you."

Ellen whispers to Anna: "Something bad is going to happen to me, Anna. There is a blood clot in my leg from God. It might kill me. The next time you see me I might be dead."

"Why would God put a blood clot in your leg, dear?"

"He's mad at me."

"For what reason?" Anna says.

"He thinks I love Michael more than Him."

"Michael," Anna says dreamily.

Sometimes Anna drifts away when Ellen is speaking to her. Sometimes, Ellen thinks, Anna's head is stuffed with wet cinnamon as hard as stone; words can't get past it. Grandma Chiradelli sometimes plays a game with Ellen to help her sleep: she makes Ellen imagine that her head is filled with cinnamon or sea water or night and then she says one word over and over and it makes changing patterns like a kaleidoscope: Bella. Serenissima. Désolate.

"Anna," Ellen whispers. "Help me, Anna. I don't feel good. I don't feel right."

"Papa seems to be searching for you, love," Lucia says.

Ellen looks up and sees Sam walking among the tables looking right and left. He might never find her. If she stays very still she is a shadow. She and the aunts are as invisible as dreams.

Ellen goes up to him and he tells her it's time to eat.

Oh how Ellen hates peas! There are fifty-six of them. She arranges them into a circle in her flattened mashed potatoes. Now they are pills, like the pink ones her mother takes from a blue plastic case each morning. Ellen swallows them whole, one at a time, with a water. When she takes them all she will be fifty-six days older. Inside each pea is a princess.

A man outside on the bocci lawn is smiling at her. Ellen has seen him several times before and he has never ignored or given her mean looks. He is one of the players and though a little old—forty, Ellen guesses—he is very handsome. His eyes and hair are dark and he is tall. She watches. When it is his turn he throws the ball too hard and it knocks against the little white one. He looks over at Ellen again, smiling, and she dimples back.

"Who got married anyway?" Sam says, looking at two men in tuxedos who have drifted outside to watch the bocci games.

"Vito Del Greco's daughter, Rosa, and Sal Benedetti," Nina says.

"Del Greco . . . with the six daughters?"

"That's right," Nina says. "They sit two rows ahead of us in church."

"Which one is Rosa?"

"The ugly one," Ellen says.

"Oh, yes," Sam says.

"Vito's wife is in my aerobics class. She said if we happened to be at the club tonight to stop in at the reception for a drink," Nina says.

"You said Mrs. Del Greco was a bitch," Ellen says.

Nina looks over at Ellen. "I most definitely did not say that."

"You said it last Saturday at the mall. You told Mrs. Genovese that Mrs. Del Greco was a ball-breaking bitch."

"I'd like to stop in and say hello," Nina says.

"No," Sam says.

"Why not?"

"Because I am fighting with Del Greco's pansy cousin, the florist."

"I insist," Nina says.

Ellen slips away while her parents argue to make her rounds in the ladies' rooms on the first floor and basement. She puts five or six tracts on the back of each toilet, a stack on the vanity, and slips one beneath each carefully folded towel. But she still has so many, even after leaving double her usual amount.

She pauses at the men's bathroom. Saint Teresa would probably do it. She puts her ear to the door and steals in when she doesn't hear anything. She stops and stares at the urinals. Planters, she guesses, except that there isn't any dirt inside. Artwork: standing back she sees that they are long faces, the jaws dropped down in shock, the mouth with a little pool of water inside. They are her parishioners, lined up and waiting. She moistens the edge of the pamphlets in the mouths, sticks one to each forehead. She is a priest. It is Ash Wednesday.

Nina and Sam are still at their coffee when Ellen returns. And the bocci players have come in. They are at a corner table opposite the aunts. The player who noticed Ellen earlier is looking at her and smiling. She saunters over.

There are seven players including the smiling one, who is the only one paying her any attention; the others are discussing something intently in Italian. She slides into the booth next to the one who smiles, sits as close to him as she dares. He asks her name.

Usually she invents a name for herself when strangers ask, but there is something about this man that makes her give her real name, as though she believes he will know if she is lying. She says, "Elena Serafina Capalbo Chiradelli."

"Those are a lot of names."

"Papa says I'll grow into them. My confirmation name is going to be Teresa. Then I'll have five names. When I get married I'll have six and if I get married twice I'll have seven then when I die I'll need a big headstone."

"Very true," the man says.

Ellen searches his salad for olives.

"Is that your papa over there?"

Ellen looks up and sees Sam motioning for her. "No. I never saw him before in my life."

Sam walks over. "Come, Ellen. It's time for us to go."

"Home?"

"Upstairs to visit the wedding celebration, then home."

"No."

"Come, Ellen, don't make Papa angry."

"No."

"Just for half an hour. Be an angel." Sam reaches for her hand.

"No! No!"

"Have some work to do on this one, yes?" the man says. "Why not leave her here with me while you go upstairs? I'll be more than pleased to watch over her. We'll be here for hours yet."

Sam looks at Ellen. She smiles at him coyly, her eyes cutting around slowly to glance up at him. This is—was—Nina's expression, something he hasn't seen for at least ten years. Where did Ellen see it?

"You bought your Saab from us," the man says.

Sam looks from Ellen to the stranger. "What?"

"Your car. You bought it from us last year."

"Are you one of the Falconi brothers?"

The man nods.

"I'm afraid I don't remember you."

"Well, there are eight of us."

"Which are you?"

"Carlo."

"Carlo Falconi," Sam says, trying to stir his memory. "Well, it's a great car. Has never given me a minute's trouble, unlike certain little creatures." He winks at Ellen and she smiles so sweetly that it makes him heartsick. Sam turns to Nina. "Carlo Falconi," he says, but she is already moving away and heading toward the stairs. "Okay, then, I'll be back in half an hour or so. Be sweet, Elena."

"Always, Papa."

Ellen takes ice cubes from a water glass and rubs them over her eyelids. "Ice reduces swelling. I have hemorrhoids."

"You're a strange little bird," he says, and laughs.

Ellen draws up and spreads her knees, revealing her panties. From the dark corner across the room Ellen thinks she sees Lena's eyes flashing red and angry, Anna shaking her head, making the sign of the cross.

"What do you have there?" the man who calls himself Falconi says, pointing at her sock. She gives him the tracts. His eyes are so dark that when she looks in them she sees herself.

"'The Road to Salvation,'" he says and laughs. "But where do the wicked go after death?"

"To hell!"

"And what is hell?"

"The absence of God and an everlasting pit of fire." Ellen has been trained in all the correct responses.

"And how does one avoid the torments of this pit?"

"By not dying."

"Ha! Pretty good," he says, and slips the tracts into his pocket.

"You can't keep those!"

He smiles at her. His teeth are very white. "Says who?"

"Says me. Gimme," she says, holding out her hand.

But now the men at the table are quarreling about something and Falconi looks away from her. They are speaking argument Italian, something she has heard between her grandparents; it's like ordinary talk, as far as Ellen understands, but words mean more because you repeat everything twice in a shout and point at people while you say them. She sighs, drapes her legs over one of Falconi's and lies back. He glances down at her, rubs his hand over her calf. But there is a terrible tenderness there and she jerks her leg away, puts her crossed feet up on the table.

There is a pause in the conversation. "My God, whose *enfant terrible?*" somebody says.

Falconi looks down at her with his great black eyes, says, "Just a little elf that wandered my way."

If she listens closely enough, Ellen can hear the aunts talking in the opposite corner. Their voices are like the cool side of a pillow. She stares up at the ceiling. And here are the aunts now, swinging on the chandelier, back and forth, back and forth, arcing out wide and high and fast so that their hair and skirts blow back. Anna, her favorite, straddles the center chain, her legs straight out in front of her, Lena and Lucia hold onto the sides. They drop notes rolled in olives into the salads, contradict everything the men say as they swing over the table. Now the aunts and the men are singing a little rhyme Grandma Chiradelli made up.

(The men): *The moon is made of Swiss.*

(The aunts): *It's made of fontinella.*

(Men): *The angels waltz in heaven.*

(Aunts): *They dance a tarantella.*

Falconi pushes Ellen's legs away and slides out of the booth.

"Hey. Where are you going?" She follows him down a hallway where a yellow light from the lamps on the dark red walls gives everything a shadow. This is the corridor that leads to the conference rooms. She rarely visits the bathrooms on this side because people in the restaurant don't use them; she left a stack of pamphlets in the ladies' room once, and when she checked back two weeks later they were all still there.

Falconi is sitting on a bench around the corner, smoking a cigarette. "Are you trailing me, love?"

"My booklets. I want my booklets back now."

He flicks his ash into a potted palm and pats the bench beside him. "*Bella*," he says. "You are a beautiful young lady. Sit here with me for a while and I will give them back."

"Do you promise?"

He nods. "Come closer. Sit close to me as you were doing out there."

She hesitates, then does so.

"Give me a kiss and I'll give you your booklets back."

"You said I only had to sit here."

He laughs. "If you give me a kiss, I will give you five dollars."

"On the lips?"

"Right here," he says, touching his cheek.

Ellen kisses him and holds out her hand. He gives her the bill and she puts it in her sock. She lets him touch her hair, her arms, her waist, and now inside her panties. This feels good.

Then it feels better.

Any place he touches becomes warm, tingly. She feels as relaxed as nighttime in her grandparents' house. Feels like she does when she is spending a weekend with them and falls asleep on purpose in the living room so somebody will have to carry her upstairs. Then it feels like she is floating and she always hears Grandma Chiradelli's heavy step and voice behind her directing the invisible arms that bear her to the bedroom with the dark furniture and cool air that smells like cooking and leather and laundry bleach.

She is as relaxed as that now. The man's hands make her feel so good that she thinks there must be a little piece of God in them. Her skin is like breath on a cold window: thin and warm and shifting. She is in the center of a circle that swirls blue then white then blue again, and it feels like he is making the colors inside her out of her own heartbeats: bubbles rising up white through black and his hand rubbing them into blue.

I am dying, Ellen thinks, because when there is no place inside her that doesn't feel good, the circle begins to break from the center out, like layer after layer of glass. Anna's face appears smiling before her, her head covered with a mantilla. Her lips move without sound: *Michael.*

But then it stops and her skin fits tight to her again.

"Elena, Elena, you make me so sad," Falconi whispers. He turns her face up to his. "I want to tell you something you won't understand now, but I want you to remember. More than anything in life I want to be a father. But my wife can't have children. This is the closest I will ever come to witnessing the birth of anything."

He stands, walks around the corner to the men's room. Ellen follows him in, right into the stall. He looks surprised, then says, "Oh, I suppose you want your booklets back."

She shakes her head. "I want more."

He laughs. "Go find Mama, little girl."

Ellen wraps her arms around his waist. "I think I love you."

He looks down at her and is silent for a few minutes. "You are not afraid of me?"

"No," Ellen says.

But this time it doesn't feel good; everything about him seems suddenly too big, too heavy. She feels as though she is being made to swim too fast, that his arms, tight around her, are holding her underwater so she can't breathe.

"You're hurting me," Ellen says.

"Look up. Look up at the light."

She does so. Years from now it will be this light that she remembers in detail, a dingy yellow bulb through an opaque frosted cover around the edges of which are moths in various stages of decay, and it will seem to belong more to seedy urban hallways than it does here.

Her heart is racing. With one hand Falconi pins her arms behind her back, the other hand is down there, pulling at her underpants. She hears silver clinking, and for a moment thinks he is counting his change, but it is his belt buckle being unfastened, the snap and zipper being undone.

"Don't be afraid," he says. There is a sharp, unexpected pain that is as bad as someone tearing off her fingernails. She screams for Anna and he puts his hand over her mouth. She is a face on a chimney in a picture where you circle what doesn't belong. Nobody will find her for years and years. Her eyes and mouth are bricks that can't blink or speak. She might be here forever, staring at a light in the distance waiting for someone to look up and notice her.

But now she sees the faces of the aunts hovering around the light and knows from their expressions that she is not going to die: they don't look surprised or frightened. Anna's face is ordinary and tired, like after Saturday cleaning.

His body is still against her now. Ellen sits on the floor and cries. The blood clot, instead of moving to her heart, is moving out of her.

"Elena," he says. "Elena, I want to tell you something." He pulls her to her feet. "I have never done this before. I have never hurt a child before. Do you believe me?"

She doesn't respond.

"I didn't mean to do this. I took advantage of you. I want you to say you can forgive me. Not now, perhaps, but someday."

She shakes her head. "I'm telling Papa. I am going to tell my papa."

He squeezes her face in his hand. "You musn't. This has to be our secret."

"No," Ellen says.

"Sadly, if you tell your papa, I will kill him. I will shoot him tonight under a bridge. Do you want that? Do you want your papa to die because of you?"

Ellen can't speak, is mute while he washes her face, combs her hair. "Your booklets," Falconi says, and puts them in her hand. "I want you to think of what happened as a game. Like bocci with our own rules. I know it doesn't seem so now, but in the long run that's all the importance it will have."

She stands by the sink a long time after he leaves. She is cold, feels as though she is dreaming and has to imagine her legs before they will work. She looks down at the tracts. Some angels look more real than others, some have wings that look stiff, plastic. It must be that some angels are not angels at all, but ordinary men who bought their wings at Sears. God can't notice everything. Maybe some things are too tiny for Him to see. Maybe He made children small because He doesn't like them. From heaven, she must look no bigger than an eyelash.

She puts the tracts in the garbage. What she wants more than anything in the world right now is a purple crayon so that she could write her name on every smooth surface she passes.

Anna is gone, the bocci players are gone, the tables all have new faces. Upstairs, the wedding guests are in a tarantella circle. Ellen weaves in and out of legs, bodies, trying to catch her father as he dances by.

Papa papa papa. But her voice can't reach him any more than her hands can. Somebody steps on her feet. She sees Nina with her arm around Mr. Del Greco, and here is ugly Rosa with a big nose and a smile and too many teeth.

Then the music stops and Ellen feels hands reaching around her, a warm palm on her clammy forehead. She turns. Sam is smiling down at her and he seems to Ellen both too near and too far: as though his hand on her head weighs a thousand pounds but that if she called his name forever he wouldn't hear.

"You look worried," Sam says. "Did you have trouble finding us?"

She shakes her head.

"Did you see the bride? Too soon it will be your turn."

"Papa," Ellen starts.

"Yes? Why do you look like that?"

Ellen begins to cry.

"Elena, you're breaking my heart. Tell me."

"I can't," she says.

"Why? Has there ever been anything you couldn't tell me?" Sam strokes her hair and an image of herself with Nina's bra on her head—it seems so long ago now—flashes in her mind.

"You won't love me anymore if I tell you."

"That could never happen. Not in a million years."

"You will die if I tell you."

"I'll take my chances."

Ellen glances around. Any one of these men might be a spy. "I know something," Ellen says.

"What do you know?"

"God never wanted any children."

"How do you know that?"

"He killed His son. Jesus Christ is dead."

"Yes, but now He's in heaven," Sam says.

"He's in the men's room. He bled to death."

"Elena, Elena. Come now, dance with me like we always do," Sam says, and lifts her so her feet are on top of his. But even Sam's slow steps are painfully too wide. She feels a dragging pressure in her lower belly, her own blood stinging against the places where her skin is raw. Tonight before she goes to bed she will stuff her panties behind the water heater in the basement.

The band is playing a slow song and people hold each other close. Ellen sees Nina dance by with Mr. Del Greco, who is saying something to her that makes her smile.

"I have good news," Sam says. "I have settled with the florist and your carnations will start coming again."

"No," Ellen says, looking up at the musicians on the stage.

"No?" Sam says.

"Those things," she says, pointing. "I want those things that man has by the drum."

"Cymbals? What do you want with cymbals?"

Ellen looks at him. "I have to whisper it."

Sam bends down.

"I want cymbals in case I get lost. I could just stand still and crash them and you will always be able to find me."

"Elena, all you have to do is call for me and I'll find you."

"But what if I have lost my voice, too?"

Sam draws her closer and Ellen concentrates on the warm pressure of his hand, his feet beneath hers moving slowly to the music. It is this image of herself she is already beginning to remember, the firm steps that lead her around and around through the confused crowd as though to tell her: Here is where you find yourself.

Truants

It's been our secret for three weeks now. Every morning my father and I head out the door with Mom at eight-fifteen like we mean to go to school and work, but what we've been doing instead is meeting behind Cafe 401 sometime around nine, Monday through Friday. We are on vacation, Dad and I, taking a sabbatical from life.

Often we go for drives in the country or visit the Carnegie Museum and hang out near the paintings by the Romantics, but our favorite thing is to watch our neighbors through their uncurtained windows. We have spent up to an hour—no kidding—just sitting on the bench across from the Golds' apartment marveling at the natural habitat of people who find faith in daily rituals. Mrs. Gold at her ironing board, for instance. Watching her go at it with the spray starch, the sleeve board, the deluxe steam iron, you'd think there must be something more at stake than the absence of creases. Or the Healys two blocks down: the kids at their Cheerios and Civics text-books, the parents scrambling around madly while the morning news on TV serenades the bright kitchen with other tragedies, other lives.

I am eighteen this April, in my last year of high school, but because I've missed so many days I'll probably have to repeat the year. Which is fine by me. I am nowhere near ready to choose a college, to fumble around with do I want to do this or that with my life. Dad has fixed it so the school thinks I'm bedridden with a lingering infection, so exhausted that if I touched cool glass my fingerprints would be blurry and edgeless as dreams. That type of thing. He's a sales representative for McNeil Pharmaceuticals and knows his diseases.

My father and I have a history of truancy. It started when I was in grade school. My mother is an attorney who works round the clock and so on the days I was sick it was Dad who stayed home with me and turned my pillow to the cool side. We'd watch re-runs of shows like "Father Knows Best" and "Leave It to Beaver." I loved the Clea-vers at dinner. They all had the same amount of food on their plates and the world was made rational and kind again by the time Beaver asked for seconds. Dad and I slept late, watched TV, and went out for ice cream in the early afternoons.

I remember the exact day our little vacations started. I was thirteen, it was an early spring morning. My dad came into the kitchen, said: "Well, Caitie, your old Dad has a cold, maybe even the influenza." He said this as though he were announcing his retirement or some-thing. He kind of smiled at me, then nodded to my mother who said, "Christ."

The thing about my father is, when he's sick, he groans. I mean every exhale is a sound of defeat. My mother can't stand this. With her it's just take two Dimetapp and glut on fluids. She has no sym-pathy for those who must convalesce even from a bad headache. So that morning Dad was going, "Oh oh oh." And I looked at him, my spoon halfway to my mouth, but it wasn't my attention he wanted. He did it again only louder, more dramatic: "Oh. Oh God, my head," sniff sniff. There was no way my mother could ignore this and she turned to him and said, "Christ, Eric, you'd think you're the only person in the world who's had a head cold."

My father gave her this stern and innocent look, like this is how I deal with illness, take it or leave it.

She laughed, palmed his forehead for fever. "You do feel a little warm. I'd stay home with you but I have to be in court."

It just so happened that we were having assemblies at school that day. I mentioned this to my parents, said I would be missing nothing important and that I would gladly stay home with Dad. They both thought this was funny but then Mom said, Why not? It was a good day: the bright blue afternoon and my father teaching me chess, the cool air coming in and stirring the crumpled tissues on the floor. The best part of being sick on gorgeous days is the wonderful stalling feeling you get, like the day itself will help to heal you.

About a month ago, I noticed that my father came to the breakfast table ten minutes later each morning. He moved real slow and seemed confused by the smallest decisions. Like Mom would ask: Do you want eggs or oatmeal? and he would wait for me to suggest something. While Mom made breakfast, I'd slip into my parents' bedroom and pull out a shirt and tie for him to wear. Otherwise he'd be half an hour in front of the closet and Mom would get mad, not understanding how overwhelming it can be when a paisley tie matches everything.

So one morning Mom was already gone and Dad and I were still finishing our coffee and he said, "I'm sorely tempted to stay home today. All this snow and ice."

I agreed. And we sat there, taking our time, pretending not to notice the clock. Forty-five minutes later it was: "Caitie, look at the time!"

I said, "Jeepers. We're such dazers."

"I suppose I can drive you to school."

"To tell you the truth, I'm not feeling very well." That was a big lie; I felt fine. "Maybe I'll just stay home today."

He looked relieved and told me to go back to bed. A few minutes later I heard him on the phone with his secretary telling her he wouldn't be in for a few days.

We stayed home all week and on the following Sunday when he started talking about the shoddy care of the elderly in nursing homes and babies of crack-addicted mothers, I had a temperature of a hundred by evening. Anytime Dad talks disease at the dinner table I usually end up with a low-grade fever. Which is why my mother never lets him talk about his work day while we eat. Instead, we hear about this or that case she's working on, about embezzlement and misappropriated funds or how the Guild for the Blind is the latest fad among the big corporations that want a charity for a tax write-off.

The Saturday after our first week at home I was walking off bad dreams and I found Dad in the kitchen, just standing in the dark looking out the window above the sink.

He pulled me next to him. "We're such an acquisitive society, Caitie. I think it was Kipling who said that we spend the first half of our lives accumulating possessions, and the second half getting rid of them so that we can die unencumbered."

I looked up at the moon. It was yellow as a jaundiced eye and spilled a greasy light on the snow. "I can't think of anything I want to acquire," I said.

After that night we stopped making excuses to each other for not going to school and work; we just stayed home. My father has something I need. I don't know what to call it, but it's like there's this shadow at the back of my head and sometimes when I'm alone with it I feel it sinking all through me until it seems I've lived my whole life already and nothing will ever be new again. But when my dad and I are together the darkness stays high and balanced, like inside both of us are shadow magnets.

It is raining this morning, but through the sun and lightly, the kind of day where you're tricked into leaving the blinds up in the false hope that the weather will clear. Mom left for work earlier than usual, so Dad and I didn't have to go through the charade of leaving at separate times and meeting behind Cafe 401.

We don't bother to dress.

Mom has left seven or eight college catalogs on my desk, the ones from Carnegie-Mellon and Columbia—her schools—on top. She's been sending away for them for about three months now, and new ones arrive each week. Around eleven each morning I am sick with dread. I can determine what's in the mail by the sound it makes going into the box. The crisp, quick sound, *whit*, means only bills. Magazines and circulars thud slightly. The college catalogs thump like dead pigeons. I have to do two things—no, three—before I can even look at them. The first is to forget I ever saw the newspaper clipping Dad has kept in his wallet for years. It's a story about a junkie found dead in the park with nothing in his pocket but a Phi Beta Kappa key. When I think about what knowledge got that man, I start imagining college as one big soup kitchen where what they give you might or might not keep you alive. The second thing I do is pull out this photograph of myself sitting on the curb in front of our old house on Murray Avenue. I am two, bald and toothless, and look like Winston Churchill. But there's something about that picture that makes me think I wasn't always afraid of becoming whoever or whatever I looked at. Like if I could have talked I'd have said: This is the sidewalk, this is a fistful of dirt, this is my hand. When I have to walk past the bag ladies on Liberty Avenue or the winos sleeping next to garbage dumpsters, I call this picture to mind, repeat to myself, Here is the sidewalk, here are your feet on the sidewalk, here is your life.

The last thing I have to do is try not to imagine my mother's reaction when she learns that looking at the catalogs is the closest I'll get to college for at least another year.

Before I know it it's four-thirty and Dad hasn't been out of his room all day. He's still in his pajamas when I go in, sitting up in bed reading *Goodbye, Columbus*. He watches me with this distant, sad look as I pick up the wadded tissues on the floor, gather newspapers, stuff clothes into the hamper.

"Betrayal is the worst infidelity." He just states this matter-of-fact, the way someone might say, American cars are made better. I look at him and he says, "I wasn't thinking of anything in particular."

"Oh. Do you realize it's almost time for Mom to be home?" I sit on the edge of the bed. His skin smells cottony, like the sheets.

"We pretty much wasted the day, didn't we? I thought it was going to rain all day, that's why I didn't plan anything. We could have gone to the museum."

"It's nice just staying home, too," I say. Actually, we haven't done anything but this for days. We see less of each other now than when our days were separated.

He stares into space not moving, like he's waiting for his words and thoughts to have a chance meeting somewhere inside him.

"Dad, get dressed now. Okay?"

He nods. I go back to my room to change into my school clothes. Down on the street I see the actor who lives in the high-rise across from us. He's carrying a pizza and a pink feather boa. He keeps himself in good physical shape. I have a full view of his living room from my window and every night between five and seven o'clock he dances. I like to watch.

From what I've seen, he has two girlfriends: the chain-smoking blonde, and the brunette who comes later in the evening but who I think stays all night. What I can't figure is how these two ladies haven't found out about each other yet. The actor doesn't love the brunette; he's just waiting for the right moment to tell her there's someone else. He is in love with the blonde; it's clear just from the way he walks across the room, his gestures, when she's with him.

The actor has a tendency to self-exhibit, and here he comes now wearing nothing but his jockeys. Around the living room are stage lights. When he dances he always puts a colored gel over them. Tonight he uses blue.

He begins to move to music I can't hear, dancing through the marbled shadows, the blue fury. His muscles are sleek, the wings of his shoulder blades like two cocoons with the silk rolled tight. Sometimes I imagine it isn't the music that makes him dance but the light, the blue a secret sorrow he wants to shed.

Dad knocks on the door and walks in. He's dressed in his work suit, his tie half-unknotted and the collar buttons on his shirt undone. This is his I've-been-home-about-twenty-minutes look, the interval of time between his arrival and Mom's.

"Well, I see Mr. Broadway's home," he says, looking at the actor. "God, the things people do in front of windows."

The actor is dancing now like he wants a woman beside him.

"That walks a tightrope with obscenity," says Dad. He looks back to me, glances at my clothes. "I don't care for those jeans, Caitlin, they're much too tight."

"These are just my school jeans."

"Too tight." His face brightens. "We can go shopping tomorrow. We'll get you some new clothes at Kaufmann's."

Dad prefers me to look like Little Bo Peep: lacy blouses with pearl buttons, fully lined skirts in case I turn sideways in the sun.

"We should probably get on out there," he says.

We head into the living room, where he drapes his suit jacket over the chair by the door, puts his open briefcase on the coffee table.

"Is everything pretty normal looking?" he says, and glances around.

I say I think so, and open the windows so our hair and clothes will have an outdoor, weathery smell.

Dad flips on the TV without volume and puts a Bach album on the stereo. He sits almost in profile to the set so that he catches the images from the evening news out of the corner of his eye. Right now a murder victim from the Hill District, Pittsburgh's worst neighborhood, is being sheeted and wheeled away to "Sheep May Safely Graze."

I open my history book when we hear keys rattle outside the door.

In breezes Mom. "Hello, hello," she says, kicking off one shoe by the door, another by the wet bar. She's gorgeous, my mother. A former Miss Pennsylvania, scholarships to Carnegie-Mellon and Columbia, Phi Beta Kappa, perfect hair, intimidating wardrobe, never misses a day of work. On the weekends she does consulting work for the Student Legal Aid Services at Pitt.

She pours a glass of Scotch. "How long have you two been home?"

We say: "About twenty minutes."

"Un-huh. And somebody's a big liar."

We look up.

She's holding out an ashtray crammed with butts. "Five, six . . . nine cigarettes in twenty minutes. You told me you had cut down. And don't tell me these are left over from yesterday. I just emptied this before I went to work."

Dad looks at her then at me.

"Well, some of those are mine. But I'm not going to smoke anymore."

"That's right, sweetheart," she says, walking into the kitchen.

Dad glares at me, though I don't think he intends the look to be mean. This is just the hardest part of the day, when Mom comes home and Dad and I have to invent our lives. It's like what an actor does to get into character. I list: Grades. Boys. Who might ask me to the senior prom. Mom will ask about these things and I have to pretend they matter, convince myself that I am still young.

Mom calls us into dinner. She puts candles on the table, turns on the stereo. She goes through music phases: a month ago we listened to nothing but jazz, then it was avant-garde until John Cage gave us all indigestion. This evening it's Louis Armstrong singing "What a Wonderful World."

We sit.

A silence slides down. Mom pours herself a big glass of wine. Usually she's the one to start the dinner conversation, but tonight she doesn't say anything, which means Dad and I have about three minutes to offer slices of our day before she becomes suspicious of the quiet, knows that we are accomplices in each other's silence.

"I had a test at school today." Mom looks at me now, coming back from wherever she was. "I was caught cheating."

"You're kidding." She looks a little panicked, her eyes bright and wide open. Though it might be from the wine. "You are kidding."

"It was a current events quiz. I copied the answers from the boy sitting next to me, some digit-head with a pocket protector. The teacher sent me to the principal's office and he almost suspended me. Except that I don't have a prior record so he let me off with a warning. He was really nice about it. He goes, 'Caitie, why would an honor student, a student who has been in advanced placement classes since junior high, cheat?' And I said that I just wasn't prepared, that I hadn't been sleeping and couldn't concentrate very well."

Mom stares at me. I don't dare look at my father. "Pass the salt," I say.

"Is that true? Are you having trouble sleeping?" Mom says.

"She's been staying up too late watching television, haven't you, Caitie?"

I shrug in my father's direction but don't dare catch his eye.

"Why didn't you tell me you were having trouble? If you have a problem, you need to take care of it."

"Things are okay now. I won't do it again. I'm not a cheater by nature."

"I know," Mom says, and pours another glass of wine.

A few minutes go by. Dad says, "My blood pressure is dangerously elevated. I had it taken today at work."

"So have another cigarette, why don't you. Did they tell you to stop smoking? Cut out salt? What?"

"Usually acute onset hypertension doesn't have to do with dietary factors. It's stress, depression sometimes."

"So? Or, and?" Mom says.

"That's all. Just try to relax, not let things get to me so much."

"What kinds of things?" I ask. "What kinds of things make you depressed?"

"Oh, nothing in particular, I suppose. Everyday things. Let me have the salad, Caitie."

I hand the bowl to him. He hesitates before taking it, like he wants me to look at him but I won't. I stare past Mom at the patches of late afternoon sun on the carpet, listen to the street noises outside. Somebody is laughing. I think it might be the actor's brunette girlfriend, the one he is only pretending to love. When she comes over, he barely lets her get in the door before he fucks her, slides her out of her clothes and right into the glossy harness of sex. One time he had her up against the wall next to the hat rack with the Charlie Chaplin bowler hung on it. I saw the whole thing. Thought the entire time, what if the blonde woman could see all this? The actor would be the big loser, of course. The women would realize what a lying sleaze he was, maybe become good friends who conspire to make his life as miserable as he deserves.

Mom speaks suddenly. "You don't think I should call your principal, do you Caitie?" She pours another glass of wine.

"Everything's handled," I say.

"Linda, that's your third glass," Dad says.

She looks at him. "Count four, because I'll probably have another before we go to bed." She turns to me. "I'll call your teacher if you want. Smooth things over, make a donation to the PTA."

"Since when do you drink with dinner?"

"It's all straightened out now," I say.

She nods, then says to Dad, "Hard day. Hard week, in fact."

"Why? What's happened?" Dad asks.

She shrugs. "Nothing. Nothing out of the ordinary. Just lots of work." She stacks the plates. "Is there anything good on television tonight?"

I am still wide awake at two in the morning. I sit by the window in the living room to watch the night. Sometimes I feel like this is my whole life: sitting and waiting, waiting, waiting. For what I don't know. But I'm a believer in secret shapes: a place inside yourself where you go when you want to keep the world out. Mine is a Chagall blue, an inverted triangle surrounded by darkness. This is the place I imagine myself when I hate the world, hate the skin of strangers pressing against mine on the subway, the old ladies who carry their clothes in paper sacks to the laundromat. The place I go when the films in Biology class show kittens hooked up to electrodes so that when they approach the mother cat to nurse, they're given shocks that make them convulse and foam at the mouth all the while the narrator is droning on about learned helplessness, aversion reaction. Sometimes I imagine that everybody is secretly wired like these kittens, afraid of looking too long at another person, or touching. I suppose it has to be this way. Otherwise nobody would be able to ignore someone's misfortune or sadness, turn off a respirator, fight in wars.

Dad walks into the living room. "What are you still doing up?"

"Couldn't sleep," I say.

He sits beside me on the window seat. "I want you to know something, Caitie. Your mother and I have a good marriage. She's a woman to be admired and respected."

I nod.

"Which is why I want us to stop this little charade. It's not fair to anybody. I've been selfish. Dragging you into my gloom."

"You haven't done that," I start to say, but he holds his hand up, doesn't want me to defend him. This is what my mother calls the self-prosecution of the guilty. She says you can't come to the defense of a man who has already jailed himself in his own head.

"Just the fact that I allowed you to stay home from school was selfish. I should have insisted that you go. But I liked having you home with me, wanted you here with me."

"I want to stay home. There's nothing at school for me. I don't want to go to college right now. You didn't go till you were thirty."

He sifts his hand through his hair, kneads his scalp with his fingertips like he's trying to loosen his thoughts. "I worry about you. Everything for you is still ahead. I want you to think good things, positive things."

"Like what?"

He pauses. "I want for you to feel happy sometimes."

"I do. I'm happy sometimes."

"Not enough. I see in you what I see in myself and that scares me."

"What do you mean?"

He picks up the napkin rings—solid gold—on the end table and works one on every finger. They glint in the light from the street lamp, shiny, fierce as brass knuckles. "I'm afraid that the ache inside you will keep you from the best part of yourself."

I look away, not wanting to see the expression that goes with these words.

"Well. At any rate, I think we should finish out the week and go back to school and work on Monday."

"It would be stupid for me to go back. I've missed so many days already that I'll have to repeat the year anyway."

"Maybe not. There's always summer school. And I want for us to tell your mother together. We'll go to her office Friday evening and tell her there. Maybe take her out to dinner."

He kisses me goodnight.

Dad and I spend the week mingling with the lunch crowds on Fifth and Walnut, watching the little kids in the fenced-in playground at one-thirty recess, updating my wardrobe with blouses and skirts from the spring sale at Kaufmann's.

But Friday at breakfast we're both so nervous that Mom notices, says, "Is everybody all right this morning?"

Fine, we say, pass the muffins.

"Caitie, you look a little pale. Are you sure you're okay?"

"Fine, fine," I say.

"Fine, fine," she mimics, "we're the *fine* family. High ho, glad to be alive." She flips on Louis Armstrong's "Wonderful World."

We eat.

Actually, I am not so fine. Last night I discovered that what I thought was love was only a rehearsal: the actor's blonde girlfriend is really an actress. I was watching as they were having some kind of passionate exchange and she forgot her lines. She read the rest from a script.

When Louis gets to the second verse, the part where he sings about rainbows and friends shaking hands saying how much they love each other, Dad gets up to leave. "I have to be at the office early this morning," he says.

"Fine," says Mom. "I have to be in court next week so I doubt I'll be home before eight or nine this evening." She turns back to me. "Do you have plans for tonight?"

I look at Dad. She looks at Dad. Dad looks past the both of us.

"What? He knows if you have plans? Can't you answer for yourself, Caitie?"

"No. No plans."

Dad was supposed to suggest that we meet Mom at her office tonight. But either he forgot or he just lost courage.

"I was just going to say that the two of you should plan the weekend without me. I'm working straight through Sunday."

"Fine, then," Dad says, and walks out. I've no idea where he's going; it wasn't in our plan for him to leave like this. Last night we talked about going to a matinee.

Mom stops eating when Dad is gone, stares past me to the window. Outside the day is bright and blue with a frosty sun.

"Earth to Linda," I say. "Come out come out wherever you are."

"I'm here," she says, smiling.

"What are you thinking about?"

She shrugs. "Nothing really. Just how long the day's going to be." She frowns at my shirt. "Where did that blouse come from?"

"Oh, this? Gimbel's. I bought it at Gimbel's about a month ago." It's one Dad picked out for me yesterday, a white sea-island cotton with a Peter Pan collar, trimmed with lace and blue piping. "Do you like it?"

"Not especially. You look about thirteen." She touches a strand of my hair. "I'll make an appointment at Zigarelli's to have your hair done. Ask Arnold for someone to do your makeup, too. You should have learned these things by now."

She seems to go away again, lose herself in her own thoughts. She looks old this morning, her face dragged down. "Mom," I say, "what's wrong?"

"Nothing, Caitie. I'm just under a lot of stress at work. This case I'm working on saps all my energy. My client owns a string of nursing homes and was charged with embezzlement."

"Did he do it?"

"You bet. You bet he did. I knew he was guilty a half an hour after he walked into my office. He's a pig, actually. I know he's guilty, and he knows I know. But we both pretend not to be enlightened."

"Why don't you tell him you know he's guilty and refuse to represent him?"

She laughs. "Right. Why not? Do you know how much money we're talking about? This is the kind of client whom I'd charge ten thousand to probate his will. And, anyway, what do you think would happen if I resigned the case? He'd just get another attorney. He has enough money to be innocent, believe me."

I wonder suddenly if the judges who crowned her Miss Pennsylvania twenty years ago had guessed this about her, that there was more to her than a beautiful face and an ambition to be a mother. I've seen the home movies my grandfather—her father—took of the pageant. Mostly she looked bewildered. Kind of dreamy, unlike now where she can have an assessment, an opinion, and a solution in three minutes.

"I've been feeling a little guilty," she says. "I feel like I don't know anything about your life anymore, who—or if—you're dating, what colleges you're considering. God, commencement is in a couple of months, isn't it? We'll have a big party. Why don't I see your friends around here anymore? What happened to Emily and Amy? You three used to be joined at the hip."

"We can't have a party. I won't be at graduation."

"Sure you will. I know all that fanfare seems silly now, but you'll be glad you went fifteen years from now. I didn't want to go to any of my ceremonies either."

"I'm not going to school." All of a sudden the kitchen seems too bright.

"Are you sick?"

I nod. Something in me wants to tell her now, without my father, just let it slip out and let Dad be the one who's surprised.

"Well, why not just stay home today. Do you have a test or anything? I'll tell you what," she says, reaching for her purse. "Take my credit cards and if you feel better this afternoon, go out and buy a dress for commencement. White's always nice. Just make sure it's something you'll wear again." She tosses the cards on the table.

Dad comes home about two, having spent the whole morning at Cafe 401, doing shots of tequila. He seems more giddy than drunk, a little frantic. "We need to make this a good day. This is our last day together," he says. "From now on, everything moves forward."

We get a take-out lunch at Rhoda's Deli and go to Schenley Park, where Dad gives a mime twenty dollars to stay the hell away from us.

Dad suggests that we go to the children's museum. He wants to show me the echo booth, he says, a place he came often as a boy.

At the entrance of the booth, Dad tells me, "When we get inside, you say something. You'll see what happens." Inside it is dark and cool. Dad nudges me. But I can't think of anything, can't think of a single word I want to hear echoed. Dad begins to sing "Heart and Soul," and I join in when he gets to the second chorus and our voices divide, double, and double again until there is so much sound around us that we are quiet for five minutes before the echo of our voices dies away. When the silence settles again I whisper, "Alive," and then say it again, louder. Hearing the word domino, I imagine that the air has had my voice in it all along and it is by lucky accident that I found it here.

I am feeling pretty good by the time we get back home. Dad, too, is in a good mood. He makes the dinner reservations at Tambellini's and whistles as he dresses, which he does too early: it is just four o'clock and he's ready for the evening. He paces. Reeks of cologne. Hovers near the door like any minute his prom date is going to burst in, gowned in green polyester and borrowed accessories.

"Dad," I say, and he turns back from the hall mirror. His face is flushed and I know he must be sweating inside that flannel suit. I was going to tell him not to be so nervous, but as soon as he looks at me I feel my own palms begin to sweat. Dad once said that he and I re-define the sympathetic nervous system: he's feeling tense, and I get the headache, I'm feeling anxious and he takes the Xanax. "I wouldn't use so much hair gel if I were you. People don't use that stuff anymore. You look like you've been caught in an oil slick and that's the first thing Mom will notice."

"You think so? I just want for us to look our best tonight. This is kind of a milestone, don't you think? From this point on we share things as a family. No more deceit. No more lies. Right?"

"I guess so."

He towels away the gel until his hair sticks up all around in spikes making him look like some kind of wild Beethoven.

"Why don't you go and change now. I bought you a new outfit. It's on your bed."

The skirt is a mini, a black jersey knit tight across the hips and rear. The top matches, and is cut in such deep V's that I can't wear a bra. Dad looks up when I walk into the living room. "You look beautiful, Caitie. Here." He opens a velvet jewelry box. Inside are Mom's garnet earrings and necklace. He fastens them on me.

"I can't wear these."

"And why not?"

"Because they're not mine. And they're gaudy. Only Mom looks good in them. Don't you think garnets are a little dramatic?"

But he's not hearing a word I'm saying. He steps back and looks at me. "Gorgeous. I can't believe how grown up you look. People are going to think you're my date," he says, and laughs.

It is seven o'clock before we get downtown to Grant Street where Mom's office is. The parking lot in back of the building is empty except for Mom's BMW and a red Porsche right beside it.

She is on the ground floor, and you have to walk past her window to get to the entrance. Dad and I walk slow, like we're both waiting for the other to stop and look in. "Oh, why the hell not? If I can watch my neighbors, I can watch my own wife," he says.

We press our faces to the glass, squint through the narrow slats of the window blinds. She is sitting at her desk, profile towards us. She holds her head in her hands and is still. Paper and folders and crumpled Kleenex litter the floor. "What's she doing?" I say.

"Just resting, I guess," Dad says.

But then we see her shoulders begin to tremble, see her face as she reaches for the box of tissues. The window glass is so thick it keeps all the sound on her side, but it's a terrible thing, a terrible thing to know somebody is crying and not be able to hear it.

I turn to Dad, but he's not even aware of me; he stares at Mom with this look, like she's someone he remembers but not well. Mom looks in the direction of the window and for a moment I think she sees us, but her expression, that bewildered, dreamy look I saw in those old home movies, stays the same; her eyes translate her solitude back to her.

"Wait here," Dad whispers. He goes inside.

I watch her face change when she hears the knock on the door: panicked, then blank, and now setting into the hard edges we're used to.

Dad's face is pasty against his dark suit, and with his weird hair looks like a younger, awkward version of himself. From the way their bodies move, their gestures, I guess what they're saying: She asks what he's doing here. He shrugs, says he came to take her to dinner. Now he must be asking her what's wrong because she is nodding toward the stack of papers on her desk. He grabs her elbow and makes her turn to face him, kind of like the way the actor did with the blonde woman, the actress. Dad holds her face between his hands, wipes with his thumbs the smudges of mascara beneath her eyes. He is saying something to her, and I'm thinking: he's telling her. Telling her why he's here and any minute they will look toward the window and wave me in. But they just stand there, bodies close but not touching.

Dad watches her as she gathers up her folders, her briefcase. He glances at the window, but his face doesn't show anything, like he's forgotten there's something more than trees out here.

I'm standing beneath the street lamp next to the car when they come out. Mom looks down at my clothes and gives me a curious, weary smile. Then hostile: "What are you doing with my garnets?"

I look at Dad and he looks from me to Mom, says, "They went with her outfit." Like taking them from her jewelry box had been my idea. "You'll be careful with them, won't you, Caitie?"

We get into the car and I'm crammed into the back seat along with the junk my father lets collect back here: the fast food cartons, cigarette packages, samples from drug companies. His eyes meet mine in the rearview mirror and they look farsighted and empty. "Is everything all right?" I ask.

Fine, fine, my parents say.

We drive in silence. Any minute now Mom will notice it, ask what's wrong, and Dad will fumble and tell her the story of why we're here. But the quiet settles over us like a heavy blue lid.

Mom reaches her hand across the back of the seat, touches the ends of my father's hair. The diamonds around the face of her wristwatch glint and wink in the dim light. He half turns to her and smiles, like he doesn't remember or care that I'm back here, that we're supposed to be telling her how we lied, how sorry we are. Like I'm not part of this. Like I didn't see my mother crying, too. What does he think, that as soon as he walked into her office the view closed over?

I lean forward, close my fingers around her wrist. The diamonds on her watch cut into my palm and shock against my skin. She turns to look at me, raises her eyebrows. "Yes?" she says.

"Did he tell you?"

"Tell me what?"

I catch Dad's eye, he shakes his head slightly.

"What? Tell me what?" she says, looking at Dad.

"Tell her," I say.

"Not now, Caitie," Dad says.

Mom looks at me again, a little of that dreamy sadness coming back to her face. I feel a blue fury all my own. "Dad and I wanted to tell you," I start.

"Yes?" she says.

"We're liars. None of us is who we say we are."

Keeping
the
Beat

"Three generations of hot babes looking for love," my grandmother says, putting her arms around me and my mother, Grace. We are crowded in front of Gram's bedroom mirror getting dressed for our dates. Tonight is a kind of emergency dinner party—the third this June.

My grandmother cooks for hours each day in quantities that would have once satisfied her husband, eight children, and perhaps all of their friends. Homemade pasta. Elaborately marinated chicken dishes. Hundreds of meatballs.

Gram is a disciplined cook, keeping the same hours I used to when I had a practice schedule: eight to noon five days a week, all day Saturday. Occasionally, when she's trying a new recipe, she starts even earlier; I woke up at six one morning last week to the smell of a thick, sweet cream and melted chocolate. How well I know how this feels: making a French cream cake at the break of dawn is not unlike waking up and facing Saint-Saëns—who wants to play in D minor first thing in the morning? It's like having brandy with your cereal. I am of the opinion that, other than kissing, anything French should be saved for later in the day.

"What do you think, pearls or beads?" Gram says, holding up necklaces in the deep V of her dress.

"Neither," I say. "Bare skin."

"Oh, sure," Gram says, "I'll just be Miss Cleavage, USA."

"Beads, then."

She nods, looks at Grace scowling at herself in the mirror. "Mother to Gracie," Gram says, cupping her hands like a megaphone. "It's time to get a personality."

"Don't badger me, Mother. I don't have any patience or humor today."

Grace, of course, doesn't see Gram's cooking the way I do. To her, Gram's obsession with food is "sublimation of the simplest kind" (how many kinds are there?), something that took root after Grandpa Griffin died a year ago. Grace wants Gram to get help, see a counselor to assist her in Grief Management. Grace has recently returned to school to work on her PhD in psychology—child psychology, God help us—and has a tendency to inflict her education on us all.

I have been staying in Pittsburgh with my grandmother for two of the four months since I dropped out of music school. I have a little something my teacher calls "musical autism," the same something that Grace, furious that I'm deviating from the Career for which I've been fast-tracked since the age of eight, defines as "Malingering" (read: Laziness). Whatever you call it, I haven't produced a stitch of music for half a year. Not wanting to be assigned a "condition," or God forbid, treatment plan, I have let Grace believe it's love trouble that has interfered with my music. Which is not entirely untrue: a three-year relationship shot to hell after I found my boyfriend in bed with an oboe player.

But I can't think of these things now. Anyway, men are like buses: there'll be another along in just a few minutes. *GRReyhound!*

"Promise me something, Mother," Grace says.

"What's that, my Little Hatchet?" Gram says. This has been

Gram's nickname for Grace since she got a Mexican divorce from my father, severing all ties in one quick stroke. This blow-your-hair-back-who-was-that-masked-man? briskness is something new in Grace; my father, having had an affair, found himself divorced before his BVDs were out of the dryer.

"Promise me, from now on, you'll do things in small, modest quantities."

"I have never done anything in small, modest quantities, dear. If I had, *you* wouldn't be here."

Grace was Gram's seventh child.

"Well, this excess with food can't continue. You're not exactly in the pink of health anymore. You're just asking for another heart attack at this pace."

Grace, poor Grace, I sometimes think, halfway between Carl Jung and Helen Reddy: everything is a Sign or Symptom of something else, and I am Woman, hear me Roar. I suppose Grace is typical of many women from the late fifties: half a lifetime spent trying to marry well, another ten or fifteen years attempting to make the faulty marriage work, then throwing it all off in the end to try to get back what was hers all along—in Grace's case a fine mind and a sense of humor which Gram and I are sure is in there somewhere.

"What about this dress?" Grace says, twirling around in a blue silk number printed with fuchsia peonies. As she moves, her clothes give off a sweet and familiar perfume. There are certain things lately that can make me morose for hours, wanting everything I lost in my life to come back. The smell of hyacinths and freshly cut grass. The sound of windchimes. Car horns in the key of A.

"You look lovely, dear," Gram says.

Grace studies herself in the mirror. "You don't think the dress makes me look too much like a PTA mother?"

"You look very nice," I say, and mean it. Grace is of late stunningly attractive. And though I despise it when people say things like "Divorce agrees with you," for Grace this is true. I am half-tempted to send my father her photograph with a little caption beneath it: "Your loss, Pal." He would die if he saw her—the aerobicized size six body, her dark, blunt-cut hair with all traces of gray gone. Who would have guessed two years ago that this beautiful creature was lurking behind the June Cleaver frumpiness, the years of yes-dearisms and dinner parties?

"Are you going to get dressed, Provie?" Grace says to me. I'm wearing a black polo shirt and khaki shorts I stole from the laundromat. I am, incidentally, named Providence, after the city of my birth—not the good fortune thing. "At least put on some lipstick," Grace says.

"I'm not into the makeup thing anymore," I say.

"I don't know why you want to make yourself ugly, Provie. You have such a beautiful face. But look at your clothes. Absolutely sexless. And you do such monstrous things to your hair."

Grace and I have been fighting about my hair for a solid two weeks. I dyed it a deep plum and cut it myself, two inches above the ear on one side, to the chin on the other.

"There's not a thing wrong with Provie's hair," Gram says. "I think it's very becoming. Every time I look at her I think of eggplants. And it's her prerogative to dress like a female castrato if she wants to."

"Thanks a heap," I say.

"Well, any man who can't imagine the body beneath the clothes won't have the imagination for more crucial things. Do either of you have any cigarettes?"

"Here," Grace says, and pulls out a pack of Salems from her purse. She sits between Gram and me on the bed and the three of us smoke in silence, flicking our ashes into the upended head of an old doll.

"We better get on down there," Gram says finally. "The boys will be here soon."

Grace and I carry food to the patio. Gram has fixed chicken primavera in an alfredo sauce, wild rice with sliced almonds, a fresh spinach salad, steamed broccoli baked in a bed of cheddar cheese, and a side dish of homemade manicotti. For dessert, there are baked peach halves, and of course, her specialty, cookies she calls bow-legged brides: a sugar dough that she cuts with a Christmas tree mold for the general shape of the dress and veil. The legs are tube-shaped strips of dough that she attaches to the bottom so that it looks like the gown is hiked up to the (spread) knees. "Obscene food," Grace calls them. "I don't know when your grandmother's mind became so filthy."

Joe Lucchesi, Gram's date, is the first to arrive. He owns an Italian grocery on the south side of town, and he delivers. He comes every other Tuesday with anise oil, walnuts, figs, Italian olives. Gram has charmed him into excess, has no less than fifty boxes of rigatoni in her pantry. Much to Grace's consternation, Joe has given Gram the recipe for pizzelles, *cuccidatis*, *fettucine con gamboretti*. He stays for dinner once or twice a week and is teaching Gram to speak Italian and to dance tarantellas.

Joe walks into the kitchen with an armload of packages. *"Ciao, Bella,"* he says, looking at Gram, smiling his approval at her dress, her beautifully made up face.

"Ciao, mi amour," she says, and opens the oven. She points to the tray of bow-legged brides, says, *"Sposa gambe storte."*

Joe beams at her, absolutely charmed to the teeth.

"Mother, there must be more than a hundred dollars worth of groceries in here," Grace says, pulling out top-grade sirloin, veal cutlets, lamb chops, two bottles of expensive wine. "You can't afford this." She turns to Joe, with a look she might give a dealer who has sold crack to a twelve-year-old Sunday-school student.

"Joe, you remember my Little Hatchet, my daughter Grace," Gram says.

"How are you, Grace?" Joe says, extending his hand.

"My mother is on a fixed income."

"There is no charge for these items," Joe says.

"We take it out in trade," Gram says, and winks at Joe. "Shall we go outside?"

"Your mother makes me happy, Grace. If she had a fondness for rubies, I would bring rubies. If she liked furs, I would buy furs. She likes food. That's what I bring. And if she would agree to marry me, I'd give her a whole side of beef." He pinches Gram's butt as she takes the tray of cookies from the oven.

"Oh, brother," Grace says.

"Grace," I say, "why do you try to sabotage everybody's happiness?"

"Is that what I'm doing? I'm so glad you have these insights, Provie. Maybe you should go into clinical work."

"Girls, please," Gram says. "Let's not ruin everybody's digestion."

"You show me no respect, Provie. If I had talked to you in your crucial, early developmental years the way you talk to me, you'd have a lot more to complain about."

"I said no fighting now, my lovelies. It ruins the spirit of the food."
Grace and I exchange looks. We all go outside, and there's Grace's date, standing under the bug light in a suit and tie. Moths sizzle above his head. His skin looks ghoulish in the blue shadows.

"Oh, Alan," Grace says quickly, "I didn't know you were here."

"Yes, here I am," he says.

Alan is one of those buttoned-down types with a Harvard MBA and a dim optimism. Grace has mentioned him to me but we haven't been formally introduced.

"I'm pouring the wine, everybody please sit," Gram says. I scan the road looking for signs of Eddie, my date, wondering if he's lost or has changed his mind. This is more or less our second meeting. We went to a movie last week, two days after we met in the laundro- mat—Gram's washer is on the blink, so two or three times a week I go to Duds 'n' Suds. Eddie watched as I stole a bathrobe from the basket of a homely, middle-aged mother of two teenaged daughters. We'd been chatting, waiting at the table for our clothes to be done. She told me the story of how she and her daughters took a weekend trip to a different city each year without husbands and boyfriends. They shopped, shared a hotel room, lives, secrets. Can we be a little more corny please? I thought, but before I knew it I had her bathrobe in my basket. Eddie had been watching me the whole time, and when the woman left he walked up behind me, whispered, "I saw you, you little thief."

I turned around, looked into a pair of absolutely beautiful eyes the shade of brown just above black. Against his pale skin they seemed to shed their own kind of light.

"Do you make a practice of stealing other people's laundry?"

"Do you make a practice of not minding your own business?"

"Not minding your own business is still legal."

"Bite me," I said.

And he did—right on my bare shoulder. My hand went up in reflex, but he held my arms at my sides and whispered again, "I've seen you in here before, you sexy thing." He kissed me tentatively on the forehead.

Before I could think about it, I led him into the tiny bathroom beside the row of dryers and splashed water down the front of his shirt. "What a shame, your shirt's wet. Take it off and I'll throw it in the dryer with my things."

"Will I ever see it again?" He laughed. "Wild woman." He pinned me against the wall.

Laundromats are for me what singles bars are for others: something about the predictability of Wash–Rinse–Final Spin, and the merry whirl of clean clothes in the dryer fills me with a weird joy. And when none of my socks are widowed, when every dirty item I brought with me is safe and clean in my car, I am more or less giddy with expectation. Besides, Eddie is a welcome change. I've had it with love among the learned, the egomaniacs who think talent excuses negligence for other people's hearts. The next time I fall in love, I want it to be with someone who doesn't give a damn that I could play Mozart by heart at ten, who doesn't see my music before he sees me. Some gorgeous mill hunk in a redneck bar, say, whose dexterity with a pool cue makes me liquefy in all the right places.

Grace is doing her introductions now. "Alan, this is my daughter Providence, my mother Estelle, and her friend Joe Lucchesi. This is Alan Lipchitz."

"A pleasure," Joe says, extending his hand.

Gram giggles and passes the wine around. "Forgive me for laughing, but that's a peculiar name. Lipchitz."

"Mother," Grace says softly, a warning in her voice.

"Yes, yes. A toast," Gram says.

We lift our glasses.

"*Pe cent an,*" she says. "To the next hundred years."

"*Bene,*" Joe says. "Salute!"

"Lipchitz," Gram says. "Your lip shits, my ass whistles!" She goes into convulsions over this one, and we all laugh a little, despite ourselves. "Forgive me," she says to Alan. "I couldn't resist. No offense intended. Let's eat!"

"Where is your friend, Provie?" Grace says.

"He'll be here."

We start on the spinach salads. I pour another glass of wine, look toward the road for signs of Eddie. Alan, in my line of vision, keeps catching my eye and smiling. "Provie, I understand you're a violinist."

How did I know this was coming? "Used to be," I say, thinking of my violin up there in its case, as unresponsive to my touch as an indifferent lover. I've attempted to play twice since I've been here with Gram, but there is no music inside me. Since my room has a view, I sometimes just sit for hours and stare: the factories in the distance billowing ash, smokey arpeggios rising from the tinny music of steel.

"Everywhere she's studied, it's been on full scholarship," Grace says. "She won all the major competitions before she was fifteen. When she was twelve she won an international competition against kids four and five years older. They gave her a violin worth ten thousand dollars. What was the name of that violin, Provie?"

"Cheratti," I say, my fingers tingling with the memory of Dvořák's *Romanze* in F minor.

"That's remarkable," Alan says.

"Not really." I look over at Gram, hoping she'll break in and change the subject. But she's engrossed in her food, in Joe's hand moving on her leg.

"Did you go on the concert circuit?"

"Provie decided against it at the time. A wise move, given what we know now of gifted children who are fast-tracked," Grace says.

"Do you practice a certain number of hours each day?"

"I don't practice at all anymore. I'm musically autistic." He laughs, thinks I'm joking.

"Provie is too hard on herself," Grace says.

"Could you make me sound a little more simple, please?" I say, louder than I want to, and Gram and Joe look over at me.

"Hey, missy, I think you can get that tone of snottiness out of your voice right now," Gram says.

"Sorry," I say to Grace. I have quite a wine buzz going and the fury or sorrow I feel when I drink is precisely the reason I never do.

"I didn't mean to simplify your problem," Grace says softly.

"I didn't mean to be a raging bitch."

"That's better," Gram says. "There's plenty of chicken." She passes around the platter.

I take a swallow of wine and think: stay off the soap box, Provie. Nobody here wants to listen to your little speech on How Corrupt The Music World Is, how some people want to see you fail, how you're uncool if you practice every day and don't hang out in bars every night. There is a kind of stockbroker mentality in music schools—at least in the two I've attended—a perverse ambition for winning awards and places in a master class instead of a desire to play better music. It's insidious. And then one day you wake up and think, when was music ever a pleasure? What happened to joy?

I look at Alan, say, "Music School Lesson 101: music is about fourth on the priority list, after figuring out who you want to sleep with. After being invited to the right parties. After determining how lousy everybody else's music is in comparison with your own."

Alan nods. "I imagine the competition in those places is pretty fierce."

"Not as fierce as the gossip," I say, remembering last February. I had stopped socializing with the other music students when I couldn't stand to hear one more Poor Ellen story, one more gleeful comment about what Poor Ellen had done now. Ellen was a talented viola player who went around the bend a little, some kind of turmoil inside her that made her do crazy things like take her shirt off at parties and sit crying and topless in the corner. I admired her in a way; she was nuts, but it was at least a genuine nuttiness: She felt what she felt, and to hell with what everybody thought. And she was closer to making real music than any of the rest of us.

Incidentally, don't believe all that crap about how hard it is to learn music, what talent it takes to translate those little black marks on the page to an arpeggio or a trill. Technique, even with something as dense and knotty as Mendelssohn's violin concertos, is the easy part. After you have mastered the rudiments of fingering and bow position, the long practice sessions are nothing more than clearing a space inside and keeping it open. That's the part that can make you slightly miserable constantly. When you're totally open like this, anybody can walk right in and trample your heart with his dirty shoes.

The early part of last February I was playing well, better than I had in my life—even the Mendelssohn, which my teacher, Estling, compared to trout fishing with hip waders on: one false move in the current and you're sunk. But then something happened. I began to make mistakes—stupid, beginning mistakes that I hadn't made since I was about twelve, like errors in fingering and bow pressure. I called Estling at two in the morning and said, "Something is wrong. Something is happening to my music. I can't feel private enough." Later that day I went in to play for him.

He said, "You're holding too tight. You've got Mendelssohn in a half-nelson and you're kicking him in the balls." Estling sent me to yoga classes to help me relax. Gave me Chinese meditation balls to roll in my hand. I drank warm milk at night and slept with extra covers to facilitate dreams. Carried quartz crystals in my pocket to balance my energy.

Nothing. Estling called my clumsiness "kinesthetic arrhythmia," meaning that my body wasn't responding to the commands of my mind. It was nothing to be overly concerned about, he said, it would probably disappear on its own. But it got worse. I began to shake so badly that I couldn't hold my violin and I didn't sleep for a solid week. Estling called me into his office one afternoon. He said, "Provie, are you despairing about anything?" I said I didn't think so, but that I was feeling a little amorphous lately, like I wanted to wear about five extra layers of clothes when I had to be around people. "Come on, Estling," I said. "Give me the straight skinny. Tell me what's wrong with me."

"Well," he said. "I think what you have is a kind of musical autism."

"What does that mean?"

"You are afraid to speak, afraid to allow the music to speak through you. I've seen it before. It happened to two of my best students."

"Why would I be afraid to speak?"

He shrugged. "That, only you know."

"Why were the others?"

"And that only they know."

"You're a shit," I said.

"You're not going to like my advice," he said. "But I'm recommending that you take a leave of absence. Get some nothing little job, practice five hours in the morning, work with me privately." He looked at me. "Well, it's not as bad as all that. Think of it this way: the music is wiser than you are. When you've got it in a stranglehold, it leaves you for a while. This is a good thing. You'd choke it to death otherwise."

I took his advice for two months but things didn't get dramatically better. The day I left New York for Gram's, Estling had come into the restaurant where I was waitressing, a hotshot new student with him: a young Chinese woman with sheet music tucked under her arm and an expression that Beethoven himself would have grudgingly respected. I'd stopped the private lessons with Estling and hadn't seen him for five weeks. He didn't acknowledge my presence until I brought the check. "How are you, Provie?" he said.

I said, "Okay. A little on the empty side of satisfied, but okay." He nodded, said something like, have a nice life. I slipped a note written on the back of a napkin in the student's hand as they were leaving: "Lies and Deceit. Treachery and Betrayal. Good luck."

We are halfway through the main course when Eddie roars up on his Harley.

"Hot Diggity Dog!" Gram says. "Do you think he'll give me a ride later?"

Eddie saunters over, leather jacket flung over his shoulder. He is wearing denim cutoffs with the zipper down and a T-shirt that reads: "Gravity: It's Not Just A Good Idea, It's The Law." He is tan and his dark hair curls delicately over his ears. Don't even get me started on ears. When a man's ears are flat against his head, rosy and discreet as Eddie's are, I am more or less filled with rapture. This boy is delicious.

"Am I late?" he says, taking off his helmet inside of which is a bouquet of wild flowers. He gives them to Gram.

"How sweet, thank you," she says.

He looks down at the dirty plates, then at me. "I *am* late. I thought you said eight o'clock."

"No problem, we just started," Gram says. She loads his plate, uncorks another bottle of wine. He sits down beside me, smiling. I lean close to him, smelling his shower-damp hair and warm skin. "Johnny's out of jail," I whisper, looking down at his lap.

"Greetings!" he says, and pulls the zipper up. "I suppose he just can't wait," he whispers, running his hand along my leg. All the nerves under my skin feel like they are standing at attention and waving little flags. I haven't felt this way for so long that I distrust it, prepare myself for the inevitable: *I love you baby, but it just won't work.* But maybe not. There are certain early good signs with Eddie: he hasn't, for instance, told me I'm beautiful. Anytime they tell you that it always ends up being room service for two in the Bates Motel.

I introduce Eddie all around, noting Grace's expression especially: there is not a trace of disapproval in her face, and if she's feeling it, it's disguised as curiosity. She looks at him as though he's someone she half-remembers from long ago. She pours us all some more wine.

"What do you do, Eddie?" she says.

"What do I do?" he says, mouth full.

"What kind of work?"

"Oh. Well, right now I'm in construction. Mostly residential, home improvements. I do roofs, gutter spouts, soffit and fascia, that kind of thing. I've done some businesses, too. You know the art-supply store downtown? I redesigned their bulkhead for them. Made it bigger. Put their name in bigger, brighter letters."

"Interesting," Grace says.

Eddie leans forward to look at Gram. "This is the best chicken I've ever eaten."

Gram beams at him; she is Eddie's forever. "Have some more," she says, heaping his plate with a portion that we all laugh at.

"Great. I'm starving."

"Bless your heart. The third sweetest phrase in the English language."

"What are the first two?" Joe says.

Gram pauses, says,"'I love you.' And, 'I think we can afford it.'"

We chuckle.

"Eddie's in a band," I say.

"Really?" Grace says.

"They're called Pit Bulls on Crack."

"What do you play?" Grace says.

"Bass. Also vocals."

Alan speaks suddenly. "I was in a band in college." His face brightens; this is the first real interest he's shown in anything all night. "I played banjo. It was a folk band. We did a lot of Joan Baez. Joni Mitchell."

Grace flashes him an impatient look, then her face softens as though she, too, is remembering the singers, hearing some distant music.

"Joni Mitchell. Yeah, I've heard of her," Eddie says.

"We were called The Robin's Eggs." He laughs sheepishly. "Well, there's a story behind the name. See, we were all Phi Beta Kappa, eggheads, you know, and two of us were in love with a woman named Robin."

"That's cute," Eddie says.

"What kind of music do you play?" Grace asks Eddie.

"Hard rock mostly. That reminds me," he says, taking some cassette tapes from his jacket. "I brought some music, I hope you don't mind. I always bring music to dinner parties, because everybody always wants it and nobody ever remembers."

"Good!" Gram says. "We'll listen to it with our dessert."

"What kind of music?" Grace says.

"Let's see." He flips through the stack of tapes. "The Cure, The Go-Betweens, The Grateful Dead, The Meat Puppets, The Dead Kennedys, Dead Can Dance."

"No songs about death, young man," Gram says. "Not while you're eating my food. There are enough elegies in the world. In my house you play songs of joy or nothing."

"*Bene*," Joe says. "Well put."

Eddie pauses. "Yes ma'am. Van Morrison—"

"Oh, Lord," Grace says. "I haven't listened to Van Morrison since I was in college."

"Here's one I think you'll like. Roxy Music. They do a remake of 'Smoke Gets in Your Eyes.'"

"That's one of Mother's favorite songs," Grace says.

"It is," Gram says. "My husband and I attached a lot of memories to that song."

"The silence is nice," I say.

"Right through there," Gram says, pointing to the stereo in the dining room.

Eddie goes into the house, and in a few minutes the music spills out. "Everybody dance!" Gram says, grabbing Joe. Grace and Alan hold each other close, sway together under the oak tree overhanging the patio. I sit still, feeling as though I'm watching everything from under a layer of glass. Eddie dances in wide circles, lip-synching the words to "Slave to Love." He holds out his hand to me. I shake my head. He shrugs, breaks in, and pulls Grace away from Alan. She is vibrant and alive tonight, relaxed in a way I haven't seen in a long time. It's nice.

As it always does, music triggers something in me, and before I can stop myself I'm thinking of early summer evenings just like this one when Grace and my father were still together. Of all the barbecues we used to have. Of the time when my father and I were building a treehouse in the backyard and he caught sight of Grace pulling weeds in the garden, kneeling in a patch of sun that brought out all the shades in her hair. He ignored the two-by-four in my hand and stared at her, said, "Oh, look at her. Look how beautiful your mother is."

"Providence, come and shine your face on me," Eddie says, pulling me from my seat. I realize that I'm listening to the music and it is actually quite good; the rhythm is strolling and aerated, nicely modulated. The song is called "Windswept," and the melody is built on a series of regressive chords that dip back down by dominant thirds to recaptivate the theme. It's a classical technique, really, something like what Beethoven used: you fragment the melody line then go backward to retrieve it, make it whole again.

Eddie holds me close and I feel slightly giddy against the warmth of him. I think of what Estling said once about music existing in the very cells, that the human body craves music and movement the way it does light and images. He claimed that every person is musical in varying degrees and the greatest composers and musicians became that way because they had too little, rather than too much music; the music wasn't inside them brimming to get out, they were inside an emptiness trying to fill it.

"What are you doing later?" Eddie whispers.

"No plans."

"Come out with me, come for a drive. Will you?"

"Okay."

Gram, sitting with Joe at the table now, motions me over. She looks pale and grim, her mouth set in a hard line. I walk over.

"Do me a favor, dear, and go upstairs and get my pills." Her hand is clutched at her chest.

"Are you in pain?"

"Just a little fatigued. A good thing. Pleasure should be tiring. Don't let your mother know."

But when I come back Grace is hovering over her, shoving glasses of water at her and patting Gram's forehead with a cloth.

"I'm fine, Gracie, really."

Grace takes the bottles of pills from me. "Here, Mother, here's your medication," she says loudly, as though Gram has suddenly become hard of hearing or has dropped a few IQ points.

"Dear," Gram says sternly, "when you get to be my age and you take as many of these things as I do, you don't call it 'medication.'

Around here it's known as party mix. I'm fine now. Go back to your dancing."

"You overdo things, Mother. You push yourself too hard."

"Gracie, please. Spare me the evaluations."

"Well, I worry. Is that so terrible? I worry about you, and if it's not you, it's Provie. I don't know what I ever did to be treated like the bad guy."

"Oh, dear. You're not the bad guy, no one thinks of you that way. What gave you that idea?"

Grace looks up at me, then over at the men, who are standing close together at the end of the table, staring at the insects flying into the bug light as though it were an exhibit in a museum.

"You shouldn't think that way, Grace," I say.

"Oh? Is that why I'm kept in the dark about things? Why I'm always the last to know?"

"Now, Grace, that's not true," Gram says.

"It certainly is. You didn't tell me you were having chest pains again. My daughter quits school for dubious reasons and is in town a month before I know it. Why wouldn't I feel as I do?"

"We'll talk about this later," Gram says softly. "Who's ready for coffee?"

"Coffee sounds perfect," Alan says.

"I'll bring it," Joe says.

"I'll help," Eddie says.

The men take a long time in the kitchen. The three of us sit in perfect silence, with exactly the same amount of space between our chairs. We are three whole notes on a staff, counting to four and waiting for the downbeat.

Grace speaks finally. "Is it true what you said about having trouble with your music?"

"Yes."

"You see, you should have told me that."

"I probably should have."

Minutes go by, and then Grace says, "I like your friend, Provie."

"You do?"

"Very much."

Gram murmurs agreement. "He has a healthy appetite. And beautiful eyes."

"What do you two think of Alan?" Grace whispers.

"He's nice," I say.

"He's very tall," Gram says. "But he looks like he might be worth the climb."

We chuckle.

"Eddie," Gram yells into the house. "How about some music? Fast, happy music."

"You got it," he yells back, and in a few minutes we are surrounded by Van Morrison and the Chieftains, the simple whimsy of an Irish jig.

We tap our feet.

Alan and Eddie bring out the coffee on a tray and Joe follows with the peach halves and bow-legged brides.

"You know, don't you, I was a girl in Ireland," Gram says, looking at Eddie.

"I didn't," Eddie says.

"And you know, don't you, what happens when the Irish hear jigs?" She stands, motions for Grace and me to follow her to a space on the lawn.

"Mother, don't. You'll make yourself sick."

But Gram begins to dance, her arms straight down at her sides, hands fisted. Her legs are still lithe and shapely. "Come on, colleens," she says to Grace and me. "This is in your veins, too."

Grace and I try to copy her steps, but we are clumsy, trip over our feet as we attempt the low kicks and crossovers. "Don't think," Gram says, winded now. "Don't look down. Your feet will watch my feet."

Alan and Eddie and Joe are smiling, cheering us on, clapping.

She is right. My feet know what to do, the rhythm of the music seems directly connected to the sinews of my legs and I am centered inside the song, feeling it as much as hearing it. I don't look down, even when I feel myself misstep, and suddenly pieces of sound are coming from all around: fragments weaving into the melody line, my feet thudding on the grass, the clapping hands, the shrilling of crickets, Gram's beads rising and falling. From these, I imagine the sounds I will hear later tonight: the noise of Eddie's motorcycle as we roar down the street, the crackling of his leather jacket in the wind. And at a point more distant perhaps, the perfect pitch of C scales rising from the dead of some night, articulate and prepared, faithful to the beat.

Ice Music

As a young man, he believed his inability to speak
had caused his deafness, that if he found his voice he could surprise
his ears into hearing. He practiced in front of mirrors with words out
of his father's manuals on precious gemstones and watch repair, will-
ing his Adam's apple to agitate *pearl* and *spring*. He'd made plans for
the day he learned to hear. First he'd listen to his mother's voice, then
he would meet a beautiful woman in the city with long fingers and
hair, whose laughter was not directed at him. And music: he wanted
to hear that most of all.

Lately Emery felt those old longings again. But this time it wasn't
curiosity—his interest in sounds that accompanied the gaudy, frantic

world had long since vanished. He wanted only to speak to his daughter in her language.

A month ago Sidney came home late one night and announced that Jeff, her boyfriend, had proposed and that she'd said yes. They were planning the wedding for the end of October and were probably going to move to Kansas. Emery was stunned: Sidney had dated Jeff on and off since she was a freshman in college and Emery liked him well enough, but at no time did their relationship seem serious. He was sure Sidney was mistaking independence for love. His surprise had slowly hardened into anger. What about medical school? he wondered. She said she was applying to schools in Kansas, where Jeff intended to do graduate work. Emery's hands had lost all fluidity:
—Too sudden. Too drastic.
—For you or for me? she'd replied.

Emery didn't say anything more to her that night, thinking perhaps she spoke out of the fullness of the evening and that she'd be more approachable in the morning. But at breakfast she brought it up again.

His hands cut sharp in the air. —Where is your young man to ask my permission? I want the suitor himself to ask me for my daughter's hand.
—And what would you say if he did ask?
—I would say no. I am not giving my consent for this marriage. You are too young. We've been planning for medical school since you were thirteen.
—And I'm still going. I'm twenty-one. I'm old enough to know what I want. You and Mama were just eighteen when you married.
—That's different. It's too soon after your mother's death to think of marrying. It's not proper.

Sidney made an odd face, let her hands fall. "Two years. It has been two years. Her death has nothing to do with this."

Emery hated it when she forced him to lip-read. —It does. I have lost a wife, I am not ready to lose a daughter.
—You won't lose me. I'm getting married, not dying.
—If you marry against my wishes then you are dead to me.

She looked stricken. Emery felt remorseful the rest of the day; he hadn't meant the words, really, only the strength of feeling behind them. But when he came home from work that night she was gone.

There was a note under the salt shaker saying she had moved in with Jeff. Emery hadn't seen her for almost a month.

Walking to work one morning, Emery thought of his wife's hands. Georgia would know what to say if she were here. He'd always envied the way her hands moved language, her signing all muscle and momentum and light. Yet what he admired during the day frightened him a little at night, made her a kind of stranger: she signed in sleep, and her hands betrayed what her eyes always hid.

—I am sick of looking into your face, but sicker at my fear of what is in your heart, she said once.

Emery assumed she meant Sidney. Mostly, she signed Sidney's name, only without her daytime anger and impatience. Georgia had never forgiven her daughter for being able to hear, insisted that Sidney use only sign language, and rejected everything having to do with the hearing world, including, finally, Sidney herself.

—Why does Mama hate me? Sidney would ask him, and Emery tried to tell her otherwise, but she never believed it. Emery didn't either, until he discovered Georgia's dream-language. Often he wanted to bring Sidney in to watch her mother speak at night, not so much the words as the gentleness with which she formed them. Sometimes she composed newsy fragments of a letter to her brother in Oregon, telling him of Sidney's ambition to become a doctor. But in Georgia's dreams Sidney was always deaf: —I am afraid, Brother, it will be difficult for a deaf doctor. How will she hear a heartbeat through a stethoscope?

Emery crossed the street now and walked into the printing firm where he worked. He couldn't accept this, Sidney's marrying so soon. And this young man, Jeff, who was studying "architectural history," what kind of life could he provide for her?

—He will design buildings? Emery asked once, but she shook her head no, explained that he analyzed the ones already erected. He hoped to teach.

"Architecture as a reflection of societal and cultural change," Sidney said.

What kind of earnings would he get from staring at brick and glass?

Emery wondered, and why wouldn't he have ambitions to build? Sidney was too advanced for him.

Emery walked over to his friend Marty at the rotary trimmer. —My daughter, the future doctor, thinks she is in love with a boy who wants to figure for himself why skyscrapers are on the planet.

Marty smiled, and Emery watched his friend's hands. They were always coated with black ink and looked, when he signed, like two misdirected ravens. —The young man is a hearing, I suppose?

Emery nodded. Often his friends forgot—and it pleased him in an odd way—that Sidney could hear. Her signing, learned from childhood, had none of the peculiar pacing that identified adult learners; acquiring the signs and knowing the language were two different things.

—She met him at the university, Emery said. —He pays his own way. The daughter of deaf parents, smart enough to win scholarships, wants a man who was born into everything but has to pay for knowledge. Senseless.

—And what kind of man would be suitable in your opinion? Marty said.

—One who would wait until I die to marry her.

—Has she still not returned home?

Emery shook his head.

—Go to her. Go and talk to her. Bring her home.

Emery shook his head.

—Do you want to lose her? You will lose her, being so stubborn. Did you think she would never fall in love and marry?

—She is not in love.

—I raised three sons, all married now. It's not so bad. They come around.

It's hardly the same, Emery thought, Sidney is half my world. —This is different. A daughter is different.

Marty shrugged. —Only in that she's yours.

Emery sat at the kitchen table until late into the evening. The dog nosed and circled at his feet. He remembered that he hadn't fed her—Sidney always took care of that—and, in fact, hadn't fed himself; Sidney had always taken care of that, too. He put down a bowl of dog food then went upstairs to Sidney's room.

He loved being among her things, though there weren't many. Even as a young girl she never wanted to own much, had an intuitive feel for space and light. He picked up the carved peach stones from her bureau. Emery bought these for her in South Carolina when she was eight. Sidney collected miniatures and these peach stones with their tiny worlds and careful attention to detail—the pleats on a maiden's skirt, the thready branches of trees—were her favorites.

—Close your eyes and run your fingers over the people, she said once. —You can feel them speaking to you.

Emery sat on the floor beside her. —What do they say to you, Sidney?

—They're peach fairies. They tell me if I plant the stones they're trapped on, they'll grow lifesize and grant me three wishes.

—And what would those be?

Her fingers whispered against him. —I'd wish for you to hear.

—I do hear. I listen with my eyes. With my skin.

—Then I'd wish for everybody to hear that way.

—Such would be a harsh world.

She thought a minute then said, —Then I'd wish for people to understand. And wish that God could hear instead of me.

—But you are perfect, Emery said. —The day of your birth, the happiest day of my life. All joy then, since, and forever.

It worried him that as young as she was, she felt this division so sharply, yet, he thought, how could it be otherwise when Georgia pretended the child belonged only to one world? Georgia never wanted children, but just hours after Sidney's birth she was radiant: —Just as we are, a silent. Her fingers dance already, clutching at the air for words.

Emery asked if the doctors had checked the baby's hearing, but Georgia said there was no need to confirm what she already knew. Hearing children greeted the world with curled fists, and their daughter's hands were as open as flowers.

Other than her own doctor, Georgia hadn't let anybody at the hospital know she was of the quiet world, had drawn a line through the blank for "physical handicaps" on the admittance form. She postured in front of the orderlies and nurses by reading lips and speaking in a voice that, Emery was sure from their expressions, made them doubt her intellect.

—They think you are retarded, speaking with such a voice, he said, but she only shrugged and smiled. Later, he understood that was exactly what she wanted them to believe: it was pride, not shame, that made her deny her deafness. She mocked the hearing world with it, thought silence was superior; why else would she insist on keeping Sidney locked in it? Her selfishness had even affected their daughter's name. When the nurse came in with the birth certificate, Georgia spoke the name they'd chosen for a girl: Cindy Ann. The nurse looked at her oddly, repeated back, then spelled, the name she heard. Georgia smiled and nodded, but the nurse's head was turned slightly and Emery knew it was unlikely that Georgia had read her lips. And when Emery saw the name on the paper weeks later, spelled *Sidney*, he was furious with her. —You have given our baby girl a boy's name. Now you are happy? She wasn't born with a disadvantage, so you gave her one. People can now make fun of her just as they did us.

Emery tried to call her "Cindy" for a while, but Georgia insisted that the misnomer seemed to suit their daughter and wouldn't use anything else.

At least Sidney had always known he was interested in what was important to her, Emery thought now. This sudden foolishness about marriage was just her way of testing the independence Georgia's death had allowed her.

He switched on Sidney's radio, turned the volume knob all the way up; Sidney only kept it at half. He never understood this, why she would want only half the music instead of the full quantity. If music was as good as she said it was, why wouldn't she want it all? He placed his hand over the speaker. The vibrations filled him with a cool darkness, made him see an owl's shadow skimming a brook. It was Sidney who taught him how to imagine the language of music: it was like looking at a circle in which black marbled into white, she said. The white was the music itself, the black was the silence that had absorbed all the colors of tones.

—And that's the best part, she said. —When the music has ended and the silence of it echoes through your imagination. You see things. Colors. Movement. Anything you want.

Emery asked what an echo was.

Sidney thought a while then said, —Like an innuendo. Or what you feel after you've been in the ocean a long time and can feel the movement of the water against your body for hours afterward. An echo is like a shadow you feel.

He awoke the next morning after bad dreams—shopping for groceries with Georgia, who took everything out of the cart as he put it in—desperate to see Sidney. He dressed quickly, found Jeff's address in Sidney's little book and started out.

He rehearsed what he would say to her on the walk over. He'd make her understand that she would never survive an early marriage. Jeff, too, had to understand that Sidney had a special vulnerability and needed to be protected. Now with Georgia gone, things needn't be so stringent at home, he would tell her. It was all right with him for Jeff—or any other friends she might have—to visit as often as she desired. And there was plenty of time for a long courtship.

Emery expected the usual collegiate housing: an apartment building in between a row of others, hot air gushing from laundromats on every corner, the scent of stale beer. Instead, Jeff's house was far from campus, newly painted and set respectably apart from the ones on either side.

He climbed the stairs, pressed his face to the screen. A long hallway opened out to a kitchen flooded with sunlight. Emery knocked and waited. When no one answered he stepped in, peeked into the living room (clean, sparse, and polished), and saw them on the deck outside, the curtains on the sliding glass doors parted just wide enough to admit their forms. They were sitting under a patio umbrella, in a pocket of shade. Sidney was still in her nightgown and had her feet propped up on Jeff's chair opposite her. Their expressions were the same, as though lost in the same thought. Sidney shivered a little and Jeff wrapped a sweater around her, pulled her hair out of the collar and arranged it carefully around her face. His fingers sifted through Sidney's hair as if they heard something in it. Emery felt his chest tighten. What could he possibly say with the evidence of such gestures? With or without his consent, this wedding was going to happen. He turned to go.

Back at home, his head pounded from hunger. He took a tangerine and some letter paper to the sun porch, stared at the light refracting off Georgia's collection of blue glass, and started a letter: "Dear Sidney, Please return home. Your absence has left in me a frozen music." No. Those words were desperate, melodramatic. He started again. "If you come home, I promise not to be so unrelenting. If you are really going to marry and move away, then don't cheat me out of the little time I have left with you. And, Sidney, it is not proper or lucky for a bridegroom to live with his intended before the wedding." He paused. No, that wouldn't do either. It would make her return out of pity. He began a third time, asking her to come home long enough to take care of some small things around the house. "With gratitude, your father, Emery Maxwell Daly."

A few nights later, he came home from work and found her in the kitchen. She was chopping pine nuts for pesto. In the oven was a roasted leg of lamb (his favorite) in a honey rosemary sauce. Homemade bread still cooling in the pans. A bottle of good German wine already decanted. He had never been so hungry.

She turned and smiled warily. —I am home only on the condition that you won't make me feel guilty or try to talk me out of this wedding. Her signing was stiff, unpracticed.

—I won't, he said, and embraced her. Her skin smelled of the sun.

—I've taken care of all the arrangements. It's going to be small and simple since Jeff doesn't have much family either, and we're paying for it ourselves. Everything is done and ready except for your part. She paused. —Will you give me away?

—I will walk you down the aisle.

After dinner, Emery waited for Sidney in the parlor, where they would rehearse his part. He cleaned the mirror until it sparkled, adjusted lamps around it so the glass admitted the greatest amount of light. He stood close to his reflection and examined his tongue. Such an insignificant-looking slab of muscle, the nerves like tiny invisible fingers that formed (or were supposed to) words for the ear instead of the eye. He had only to speak two words, but it seemed impossible, exhausting, like trying to move the dead weight of his arm after he had slept on it. A month ago this might have been easier, Emery suspected, before the dreams of Georgia started. Since Sidney had announced her intentions, Georgia haunted him, would not let him sleep in peace. Last night, she even excluded him from the action of his own dreams. She and Sidney were behind a glass wall that shut him out. Georgia's appearance was altered: her hair was cut short as a boy's, her fingernails clipped squarely across. She wore one of his old flannel shirts and a pair of baggy work trousers. She bent close to Sidney and their forms were silhouetted against a diffused white light. Georgia was using Sidney's idiosyncratic signing, her tendency, when she spoke too rapidly, of keeping her index finger straight when forming the letter "f" so that it looked like a "d": —The mind is just an ear for its own thoughts. We are all dead in our own way.

—Deaf, Emery said. —You mean deaf.

Neither woman noticed him, and both seemed unaware that they were malforming the end letter.

Sidney nodded at her mother, signed at a pressured pace. —He inhabits my silence and knows me there. Our love is perfect. We will conceive dead children.

Emery looked up now and saw Sidney watching him. —Are you ready?

He nodded. She stood beside him at the mirror and placed his hand on her throat. He watched the reflection of her lips ripple in the glass: "Who gives this woman to be married?"

Emery made the vibrations begin deep inside himself, stretched his mouth into a near-perfect oval, but the sound, he saw from her expression, wasn't right.

—Shorten the "I" and end it by the "d" in "do," she said.

He placed his hands on his diaphragm and tried again. The muscles of his face ached. Sidney kept her expression even, but he thought the attempted words must sound as terrible as they felt: shapeless and involuntary, a reflex of sudden injury. How could he stand in front of all those people and make that wounded animal sound?

He pulled Sidney next to him, made her watch in the mirror how the words contorted his face. —Now, how can you see that and not be ashamed?

She turned from the mirror and looked at him. —I could never be ashamed. Just do the best you can. Pretend the people aren't out there. You are saying the words only to the minister and to Jeff and to me. It doesn't matter how they sound. We know what they mean. Try it again. Just think of it as a breath with sound.

Emery shook his head. —I won't stand up there and make a fool of myself. I will use sign. Or nod. How can I use what I do not own? He turned to go. Sidney grabbed his arm. "All these years I have been using your language. Now all I ask is that you use two words of mine. Just for once think of someone besides yourself."

—You are asking me to do something impossible. How can I trust a voice I cannot even hear inside my own head?

"Trust me to hear it then."

—I am unable. The words die in my throat.

"Use your imagination. Pretend. I've had to all these years."

—Pretended what?

"That I was deaf. That I could hear only in silence."

—Wrong, he said. —You are wrong.

Where is your voice? Sidney asked him once. Where is your voice and Mama's voice? With God, Emery had said. God took our voices for His own use. But where are they? she wanted to know. They're in a safe place, he said. They are together, inside you, and singing.

He took a tablet from the desk and wrote: "I was not the one who made you pretend you were deaf. Did I ever ask you to be anybody other than who you were?"

Sidney said, "You didn't ask, no."

—Then tell me you said those words only in anger.

"I'm going to bed. If you want to speak to me, you use my language."

Emery went into the kitchen after she was gone, sat in the dark with his whiskey. He drank until he felt the alcohol melt the knot of words frozen in his throat.

He went upstairs to Sidney's room.

He couldn't see her in the dark, but made his throat vibrate with sound until he felt the hum behind his eyes, said the words, then saw them: a red line dissecting two bubbles of blue.

Sidney turned on a lamp. She lay across the bed. Emery saw that she had been crying.

—If you can hear such a voice and not feel shame, then I will forget my own.

He arrived at the church early, paced the sanctuary, thought of half-ripe pears: the bittersweet fruit made his mouth draw up to the approximate shape his lips needed for speech.

Out of the corner of his eye, Emery saw his printer friend, Marty, motion to him from the back pew. Emery walked over, his eyes drawn to his friend's hands: it was the first time he had seen them clean. Even the creases in his palm were free of ink. Emery just stared for a moment, not registering the words from the unfamiliar hands.

—Sidney was asking for you, Marty said.

Emery walked out without looking at his friend's face, not trusting his eyes to conceal what he was sure must be there: pity. Or embarrassment. As though the hands, stripped clean, had the power to betray secrets.

Sidney stood in front of the mirror in the minister's study, fussing with her gown. Her reflection smiled at his. —Do you feel okay? she said, without turning around. —I wanted to make sure you were all right.

Emery nodded, shy suddenly, in the presence of this beautiful stranger. He wanted to tell her how much she had given him. Remind her what a rare thing they had, really, this ability to share the other's separate, alien world.

She turned, looked down at the gifts he held. Emery gave them to her: the lace half-gloves Georgia had worn on their wedding day, the road atlas with a check folded and taped over Vermont, where they were honeymooning. Sidney held out her hands and he eased the gloves over her fingers.

She smiled. —An heirloom. Some day my own daughter will wear them.

Emery looked at her face. Her expression was calm, expectant, and he saw that she needed nothing from him. Perhaps it was such with all fathers, he thought, perhaps all fathers felt this helplessness. What could he say? This is all happening too soon. You are beautiful and terrifying. I am defeated and proud. I love you and good luck.

They walked to the door of the sanctuary.

—Take my hand, Daddy, the music has started.

Against his face he felt the cool, musty air stirring from beneath the eaves, felt the vibrations from the organ heighten as her bridesmaid reached the altar. He looked down at the white runway as they walked. Sidney's hand shifted on his arm, the brittle lace of her glove murmuring against his skin. He looked over. She extended her little finger on his sleeve, then after a pause, her thumb and forefinger, forming each letter slowly, lyrically: *I love you.*

Emery's hands, as though speaking of their own volition, reached up palm to palm, opened behind her bouquet of flowers: *Bounty.*

Emery stared at the minister's mouth, watched as the lips moved and said: "Who gives this woman to be married?"

Emery said, "I do." Two words, two stones, dropped from a height into still water. And from Sidney's face, he saw it was music enough.

Just two weeks. Sidney would be back from her honeymoon in two weeks. She promised him that she and Jeff would spend some time with him, a week or ten days, before they left for Kansas.

He'd anticipated the loneliness without her, but hadn't, until now, understood how complete it would feel. His empty hours felt to him ossified, his aloneness and the encroaching outside world painful, knitting together like an improperly set bone.

He brought down the television from Sidney's room and watched it every evening, something he had never done. But television with its endless flickering and movement translated in his imagination into a kind of sound, the way it used to with Sidney: watching her talk on the phone or sing along with the radio, he sometimes imagined, as he did when he was younger, that if the quiet in him settled just so, he could listen through it.

With Sidney gone even his dreams had changed: Georgia, too, had deserted him. Now the dreams, if he had them at all, were devoid of people and language. They woke him early and kept him anxious half the day. Images of water, of light shifting at unnatural angles, of white walls smudged with fingerprints that he scrubbed and scrubbed only to have them rise up through the paint again, slowly darkening like a bruise.

The first week passed with two postcards from Sidney. She wrote of the fineness of the weather, of her pleasant exhaustion at the day's end. "Please be happy for me, Emery," she added in a postscript to one (since when did she call him Emery, he wanted to know), "I am so happy I almost distrust it."

He took three days vacation from work to tend to some things he'd been putting off: he wanted the house to be clean when Sidney came back, and someone was coming to shampoo the carpets and upholstery. And he wanted to learn to do his own shopping. Marty arranged for a high school boy to come over twice a week to take his grocery list, but Emery wanted Sidney to be proud of him, wanted to reassure her that he wouldn't be a burden when she came back for a visit. More than anything he wanted to make what was now extraordinary commonplace, to say in one of his letters to her, "This morning on my way home from the post office . . ." But the first two times he went to the market by himself he panicked, abandoned his half-full cart and went home; he had forgotten how large and confusing the everyday world was.

The last thing he did was schedule someone to come and tune the old piano in the parlor. It was probably silly, he knew, unlikely that Sidney would ever touch it again—hadn't played, in fact, since she was thirteen—but it was on this old Steinway that Sidney first learned music, where she sat for many hours, her fingers flying over the keys furiously, as though engaged in an argument with it. The piano had belonged to Emery's mother, so it was important to keep it up; there might someday be a grandson, a boy who would hear the longings and dreams preserved on the worn keys, strange images sifting through him as he played: the young Sidney with her long, lyric fingers. And even earlier, a young boy sitting with his cheek pressed against the piano leg, imagining the hammers striking the wire strings inside would cause the same mechanical reaction in him, the drum of his ear taut and ready.

Emery sat down at the piano now, touched the keys. Someday he would tell his grandson of all this. Tell how he could imagine music without ever having heard it, of how beautiful his mother had been on her wedding day. Explain how, with the right conditions and willingness of heart—the commotion of feeling in him when he gazed at Sidney that day—something like loveliness could become audible.

A Kind
of April

Anna Blum works the graveyard, the only available
shift when she started this job in the sleep clinic three years ago.
Other hours have become vacant, but really she has come to prefer
these odd gray stretches—what are nights to her anyway? Waking
up at 3 A.M. after bad dreams, making a bowl of warm milk and bread,
watching the TV shows where they try to sell you things on home
shopping clubs. Such a lot of merchandise, where can it possibly be
stored? Anna imagines a great heap of junk in the TV station's stock
room: a pile to the ceiling of clothing and jewelry and fancy knives.
Balms for the lonely and lost, Anna thinks, love, religion, forty-eight-
dollar sweatshirts—it's all the same in the end. Things to fill an
emptiness.

Anna works exclusively with apnea patients at Pittsburgh's Western Psychiatric Clinic for Sleep Disorders. Medically, apnea is a cessation of breathing while one is asleep. The patient stops breathing for a period of thirty to ninety seconds, and is awakened hundreds of times a night when the part of the brain that regulates respiration has to send distress messages to the lungs and throat. "Imagine it as being like the emergency lighting that comes on when a building's electricity goes out," Anna always tells her interns. "Alarm systems going off hundreds of times a night when the brain instructs the body to breathe." A diagnosis of apnea was easy; a trained clinician could almost make it with just hearing the patient's symptoms: difficulty staying awake during the day, frequent napping from which one never awoke rested, irritability, changes in mood or personality, mental confusion, and a diminishment of intellectual functioning—especially cognitive thinking.

Apnea sufferers were the least desirable clients to work with—even insomniacs were ranked above them—they were testy, uncooperative, impatient. But Anna likes a good challenge.

Tonight she gets to work a little early so she can study her new case. There is a minor commotion in the control room: Diana, the senior technician, speaks into the microphone to the patient in the observation room.

"Mr. Silver, we are health care professionals," Diana is saying.

"And I have my modesty," the patient calls back. "I am insisting on a male nurse."

Anna walks up to the glass.

"You're here. Thank God," Diana says. "This one is yours. He wants to keep his pajama bottoms on. Won't let us touch him."

"He is an apnea patient?" Anna says, because he doesn't fit the usual profile: he is thin, and his voice, what little of it she's heard, is diaphragmatic and not nasal, as is typical of those with obstructed airways.

"He's a self-reported insomniac, but preliminary testing has ruled that out," Diana says.

"I haven't read his chart yet. Health history?"

"High blood pressure. Arrhythmia. Total kneecap replacement six months ago. Post-surgical phlebitis. Pain in the ass. Ours, not his." She rolls her eyes. "All yours, darling. I'm going home."

Anna takes a minute to study his chart before she gets him ready.

Widower, age sixty-nine. Three children. Retired after a profession as a bookbinder.

"Hello? Hello, health care professionals, I'm catching a chill in here."

"I'll be right in," Anna says into the microphone. She scans the rest of Mr. Silver's chart. Jewish immigrant, native of Germany. Auschwitz. Anna feels a queasiness flip over in her stomach then snake up her spine: Silver had been assigned to her because of this fact. Americans were coarse in their connections, childish in their assumptions. More than anything else, Anna Blum believes the integrity of a person is measured by what is kept private. Everybody has their sorrow, and to obviate it on talk shows or in support groups or idle chatter over coffee cheapened it, made it a part of the everyday traffic of living. She's felt the eyes of her co-workers staring at the numbers tattooed on her forearm, knew their curiosity, but it was her past, hers alone. They didn't wear their bad memories sewn into their skin. She couldn't look at their bodies the way they could at hers, and say, Tell me about your abuse. Your bad marriage. The times of your degradation and shame. Anna always said, Anna only ever said, "Why keep horrible memories alive? One should build a wall against the past, not a bridge."

Anna goes into Mr. Silver's room now. He is stretched out on the bed, the sheet pulled up to his chin.

"Mr. Silver, I am Anna Blum."

"Hello, Anna Blum," he says. "And I should hope you're the kind of Anna Blum who lets me keep my pajama bottoms on."

"Did anyone explain the procedures to you?"

"They got only as far as I must leave off my pajamas."

Anna explains the medical reason for this, gives him a brief explanation of how measuring nocturnal tumescence is one indicator of how much oxygen the body is receiving in sleep. She goes over what sleep apnea is, how it is diagnosed and treated.

"Medically, there are three things we recommend for apnea sufferers. The first is weight loss. Most of our patients are severely to morbidly obese. Fatty tissue in the throat can obstruct airways. Sometimes patients opt for surgical removal of the uvula, that piece of skin that overhangs the throat." Anna feels her cheeks flush like a young girl; he is staring at her so intently. "That has about a sixty per cent success rate. Most commonly, and what we would probably recommend in your case since you are of normal weight, is a C-pap machine. This is a device that is worn at night to keep the airways open. I will explain more fully if that becomes necessary."

Anna attaches the electrodes to his head and chest for EEG and EKG readings, the heat-sensitive probe under his nose to measure airflow, and the clip to his ear to record oxygen levels. The last electrode is pasted to his forehead to reduce electrical interference. She decides for now to skip wiring him for a tumescence reading.

"You want I should sleep with all these wires? I could bring in planes."

"These are to prevent blood clots," she says, sliding the cloth sleeves over his calves. "Because of your recent surgery and the limited amount of movement possible with these wires, your circulation may be compromised."

"Better my circulation than my virtue." He winks at her.

"If you need anything through the night, push the button on this panel and speak clearly. Do not get up without assistance. All of these wires are hooked up to something called a polysomnograph machine in the control room. The doctor will be in at morning."

He grabs her arm as she pulls up the sheet, and turns it over. "I thought so."

Anna stares back.

"Just as much here," he says, touching the corner of her eye, "as there."

"Goodnight, Mr. Silver."

"Goodnight, Anna Blum."

By 6 A.M. when her shift ends, only Mr. Silver's EEG seems indicative of disturbed sleep. By his readouts—EKG normal, vital signs normal—and his behavior, Anna rules out insomnia, apnea, and night terrors on the preliminary diagnosis sheet.

Under the section marked "Other remarks or recommendations," she mentions the unusual EEG reading, and suggests confining the study to just this area over the next night.

She looks at his chart again to make sure she hasn't missed anything. After hundreds of studies, Anna can usually tell the person's profession or dominating interest after looking at an EEG. Creative people or artists had printouts that looked like mountain ranges.

Theirs were the most irregular, with the highest frequency and intensity of REM sleep. Scientific minds were more symmetrical, with small, lead-in peaks before the exaggerated jags of dreams. But this, Silver's EEG, she doesn't know. She watches him at his breakfast through the glass. He seems normal enough. No bizarre behavior or evident phobias. She has twice seen EEG waves similar to this: both had been children. Both had been abused and suffered from what was termed Propulsive REM in phase four, which meant, simply, that these suffering children carried their little hells all the way down to the bone, their dreams invading the period of the sleep cycle where the brain is supposed to shut down so the body can fully rest. It was specific to children, and relatively rare: adults who were abused in childhood did not show this, neither did the most severely battered wives or soldiers with post-traumatic stress syndrome.

Of course, she might be mistaken. Which is why it was necessary to keep him and repeat the study.

At home there are messages on her machine from her daughter, Miriam—"I have wonderful news, call me immediately"—and a somber-voiced young man by the name of Harry Elsasser, who says he is a former student, and would she be so good as to return his call. Anna remembers Harry, though it has been years since she taught biology at the university. He was in four of her classes, a major who was planning to go on to graduate school. She has vague memories of seeing him after class, talking about her exciting new discoveries of mitochondrial DNA. A very nice-looking young man. His was the last face she saw that afternoon she left the university for good. He'd walked her to her car, carrying boxes from her office. Anna tries not to remember—has blocked, in fact—those months, those humiliating last months that ended a twenty-year teaching career. Her record was sterling, her student evaluations among the most favorable in the university.

At first, the provost was sympathetic to her plea of overwork and personal hardship. Her husband, Marvin, had just died, Miriam was heavily involved with drugs and had moved back home. Anna explained all this, how she woke in the middle of one night and found that Miriam had not yet been to bed, was sitting in the corner of the living room inflicting cigarette burns on herself, looking too much like familiar human wreckage.

"Mama, I am a lighthouse," she said. "Look to me to keep from drowning." Anna checked her into the hospital that night.

The provost didn't look her in the eye when he told her she must go, that much Anna remembers. What else? The provost mumbling something about unprofessional conduct, her behavior odd and unlike her. But why think of those things now?

She resets the answering machine. Harry Elsasser she would call later. And Miriam could wait also.

She switches on the TV for background noise as she walks around the apartment watering the plants. The windowbox geraniums please her: exquisite, deeply pigmented blossoms, angling now to drink in the stingy late autumn sun. "Hello, beauties," she says, pouring in the water. "I apologize on behalf of the sun. It now keeps banker's hours, like every other person in this dim city."

Harry Elsasser. She turns his name and face over in her mind. The last face she saw, the light that day of the same tone and quality of this one. She was nervous, edgy, in those days. Was there an official grievance filed against her? There might have been, it has a familiar echo. But she calls herself back. She is fine in these days, can't recall the last time she became even mildly frustrated. Her life is calm and ordered and that's the way she likes it.

She switches off the TV, goes into the kitchen to do her food. A few years ago Anna bought two food dehydrators and nearly every week since then she has had something to add to her pantry: apricots, watermelon, honeydew, even dried turkey and beef. There was very little that couldn't be dried and stored, and once thoroughly dehydrated, food would keep for years. It comforts her to have her cupboards stocked with those hundreds of plastic bags. If something should happen, if she became a shut-in or, God forbid, there was some national crisis where the food supply was contaminated, she could survive and be healthy for years on what she has.

The phone rings as she is cutting up an acorn squash.

"I have incredible news," her daughter Miriam says when Anna says hello. "I was chosen as a finalist for the Johnny Walker Comedy Competition."

Miriam has been a "comedian" for a while now. Anna knows vaguely of her appearances in clubs in New York and the local ones here in Pittsburgh, but she has a hard time believing that Miriam could be successful at this; even as a child Miriam was disturbingly somber.

"That's wonderful, darling," Anna says, hoping her voice doesn't betray her lack of enthusiasm. For the past ten years Miriam has been a waitress while she tried to make her mark as a painter, a photographer, a novelist—whatever she got it in her head she wanted to be that week. As far as Anna knows, none of these endeavors came to anything.

Anna slices the squash into small, precise squares, lets her attention be diverted, and is ashamed of herself for her indifference to her daughter's triumphs, however small.

"This is a big deal in L.A., Mother. I'm going to be on television. Scouts for Leno and Letterman will be there."

"Oh? Television? You mean if you win?"

"If I win, for sure. But they sign finalists, too, if they like them."

Maybe this is something, Anna thinks. Television, after all. "On what channel will you appear?"

Miriam pauses, then laughs. "On what channel will I appear? Are you thinking in German again, Mother?"

"Not at all."

Miriam laughs bitterly. "Cripes. You sound like I'm trying to sell you vacuum cleaners or something. Write this down."

Anna takes down the day and time of the program, and the cable station it will be on—the one that has programs of ballets and operas and biographies of famous people; Anna is impressed. "What sorts of jokes do you tell?"

"You'll have to watch and see. Keep your fingers crossed. First prize is twenty-five thousand dollars."

"I'll be watching and saying a little prayer," Anna says, and hangs up.

At dusk, she goes into the bedroom to take her rest. The streets are quiet except for what sounds like a game of baseball. Youthful voices float up through the twilight, the fluted honey tones of young boys. Anna is sorry she never had another child, never tried for a son. There is nothing more beautiful than a lovely young boy, all the outlines of manhood there but not yet filled, the long legs and bright eyes and tender skin. She listens to one voice in particular and feels an inexplicable sorrow. "Mike, my man," the voice calls. "My man,

Mike." And then faster, the syllables running together so it's like an invocation: "Mike *myman myman myman.*" Anna watches the sky, a wounded-looking but glorious color of salmon bruised blue and purple, and drifts into sleep.

Mr. Silver, the patient with the atypical EEG, has become something of a celebrity at the clinic, the way those whose illnesses resisted categorization often did. In Anna's mailbox is a note from Diana, the senior technician, saying a second EEG was consistent with the first, and since there was no primary sleep disorder, they moved Silver to neurology. "Psychiatric disorder is probable cause of patient's self-reported insomnia, nightmares, and sensation of suffocation. A CAT scan and MRI have been ordered."

Anna writes an addendum to her notes: "MRI technicians should check and double-check for subdural hematoma. Possibly deterioration of brain fitting with Alzheimer's. Temporal lobe epilepsy should be ruled out. Psychiatric workers might test for depression and anxiety disorders."

Anna puts Silver's chart back into Diana's box, relieved that Silver has been taken off her hands. She'd been dreading her shift, knowing that Silver was on her rotation. Most patients looked at the clinician the way one looks at waitresses or grocery clerks. But this man's gaze was unnerving. More than unnerving: insulting and presumptuous. He had no business prying into her personal life. Not that he pried, exactly, but he assumed a point of reference that he had no right to. But maybe she was making too much of it. It had just been so long, so long since someone looked at her, saw her as Anna Blum, and not merely as a pair of gentle hands or soothing voice or pleasant smile. Which is the way she wants it, really. What was invisibility if not the best kind of freedom? Calling attention to yourself with a limp, a stutter, a pretty face, is certain death in one way or another.

She shakes herself out of this dreamy abstraction, turns her attention to the charts at hand. The usual cases. Two new patients with all the earmarks of apnea; tonight will be an easy night. She relaxes into reading the medical histories.

Gina, one of the young interns, comes into the control room where Anna is sitting.

"Both of the patients are wired for sound," she says. "I told them you would be in to explain procedure."

"Good. Thank you very much," Anna says, and smiles when Gina continues to look at her. "Something puzzles you?" Anna says.

"You look different tonight. Pretty." Gina blushes. "Not that you don't always look pretty, I mean, but I've never seen you with makeup. It's nice."

Anna glances down at the chart in her hand. "I notice Mr. Bartoli hasn't provided a urine sample. See if he is ready to give now. And both men need blood drawn for a CBC."

"Complete blood count, right," Gina says, obviously flustered. "Will there be anything else, Mrs. Blum?"

"That's all for now," Anna says.

The night is uneventful and tedious. Anna reads several chapters of a romance novel one of the young nurse's aides left in the lounge. Despite herself she enjoys it, gives her attention to Garth and Francesca the way one does to a vase of plastic flowers in a waiting room.

At the end of her shift, she goes up to neurology on the eighth floor. Silver's room is at the end of the corridor. For some reason, this floor is ill-lit; dark and shadowy and strict in its narrowness, like a nerve pulled taut and ready against the expectation of pain. The shape and the lighting of this wing make her heart pound, her stomach flutter. She half expects someone to stop her and ask her business here. What would she say? Patient follow-up. Or, I lost something, and I think it might be up here. I misplaced my wristwatch and am going to check the lounge. But how silly. She has every right to be anywhere in the hospital, the plastic badge with her picture and name clipped to her lab coat proclaims this.

He appears to be asleep when she walks in, and she feels suddenly so foolish that she is glad his eyes are closed. She picks up his chart from the foot of his bed and stares at Silver over the top of it. He is regal and lovely, his finely shaped head showing through the thinning white hair like well-tended ivory. How the body's tissues thin as we age, she thinks, looking at Silver's papery lids, no thicker than moth's wings and threaded with the tapestry of blue veins. One of nature's little illusions: as you move closer to the final darkness, the body thins its membranes to take in as much light and sensation as possible, greedy for life till the last. Anna envies those with faith. She herself stopped believing in God when she was ten, knowing intuitively as she was herded into the midst of human agony that if there was a God He was nothing that cared enough to save any of them. Empathy and compassion, after all, were two different things: one was a voice calling to you across an abyss, the other was a voice and an extended hand.

Mr. Silver draws in a deep breath. "Hello, Anna Blum," he says without opening his eyes.

"How did you know?"

"I've been waiting." He looks at her finally, smiles. "You are lovely-looking this evening."

Anna fusses a moment with the chart, pretends to study it as Silver watches her, then walks out without saying anything more.

On the drive home, she punches in the cassette tape that she's been listening to lately, one that Miriam left when she moved. Prince, the singer is. She must play it loud. When she's stuck in traffic she rolls up the windows: one time she forgot, and glanced over at the astonished faces in the car next to her. She is embarrassed that she, a woman on the high side of middle age, finds songs like "Alphabet Street" and "Raspberry Beret" oddly invigorating.

———————

She finds herself happier these days. Little, subtle pleasures reappearing: the unexpected rediscovery of a favorite, years-old sweater in her closet. It's been so long since she's worn anything but drab gray or black. The colors in this sweater are as inviting as its warmth: a bright fuchsia and orange wool with a print of dark green leaves. The buttons are square and made of crystal. Her husband bought it for her in Amsterdam at least twenty years ago.

One afternoon, on a whim, she drives up to Columbus, Ohio, to visit the Short North Market. It is a fine day, one of autumn's little jewels with its perfect blue dome of sky and temperature so comfortable that the air seems weightless. Anna herself feels exceptionally well and rested. She speeds through West Virginia, the bright foliage on the mountains making her think of over-dressed matrons at a party, gaudy with all their finery.

At the Short North Market, she indulges herself in her twin passions: blue glass and children's chairs. She buys all the glass she finds—vases, pitchers, antique bottles—along with a solid mahogany child's rocker, circa 1900, inlaid with gold leaf and in mint condition.

Anna pulls her files on pediatric sleep studies. There aren't many, but nearly all of the sleep-disturbed children on record have histories of one form of abuse or another.

She places Albert Silver's EEG readout next to that of an eight-year-old male who had suffered the first four years of his life in a Romanian orphanage. It is uncanny how similar Mr. Silver's graph is to this one: the same exaggerated arcs into phase four sleep at intervals so alike they could have been generated by the same patient.

Anna re-reads Albert's chart. He was sixteen when he went to the camps. Even so, even if she did label him as an anomalous REM sleep-propulsive, there was no real treatment plan available: even the most disturbed child did not require aggressive medical intervention; time did the work of the clinician.

"Our poltergeist is back," Diana says, and nods toward Silver when Anna walks into the control room. "Neurological tests negative, MRI and CAT scans clean. Dr. Weiss wants a sleep diagnosis before prescribing any medication."

"How is his night so far?" Anna says.

Diana X's points on the graph. "Two nightmares so far, from which he awoke screaming. Unusual, extended REM activity. Claims not to remember dreams."

Sometime around 5 A.M. Silver's EEG goes frantic with activity; the waves are at the very edge of the graph paper. Anna goes in and awakens him. He looks at her sleepily and smiles. "Hello, my private vision," he says.

"Tell me what you were dreaming."

"I do not know. I do not remember."

"Try." She sits in the chair beside him, is quiet while he collects himself.

"There is nothing," he says finally. "Just my pounding heart."

Anna is visibly annoyed and Silver chuckles. "I must apologize for not fitting easily into one of your categories?"

She looks at him evenly and says, "All right. Your disturbances are consistent with those of a severely abused child. Do you have any insights into that?"

He jerks suddenly forward, nearly ripping out the wires attached to him. "You must ask? You of all people?"

"I don't understand," Anna says.

He is silent for several minutes then says, "Where is *your* youth, Anna Blum? What did you do with your childhood?"

Anna bristles and stands up to go. "I don't believe in childhood."

"Ha! Anna, I'm going to find you where you live. I'm going to take you out and dance with you and fill you with luscious food and kiss your endearing face and tease out all your playfulness."

"I am assigning a new clinician to your case, Mr. Silver. I can no longer work with you."

"Anna, you are my nicest thought."

"Good-bye, Mr. Silver."

"I love you, Anna Blum."

"What! You don't know me."

"What's not to know? We are all living and dying. We are all naked and clinging in the dark."

Miriam calls the night she is scheduled to appear on television. "You're going to watch, aren't you?"

"Most certainly," Anna says, bagging the chopped turkey she dehydrated the day before.

"I want to tell you something first," Miriam says.

"Yes?"

"Comedy is an art form. The most successful comedy comes from things that aren't funny at all. I want you to know I realize that."

"All right," Anna says.

"And not to take anything personally. The Jewish mother jokes, I mean."

"I understand. I wish you luck. Break your legs."

Miriam laughs and tells Anna she loves her. It has been so long since Miriam said this to her that she is too stunned at first to speak. "I love you, too," she says, hearing how false this sounds even to her own ears.

Anna busies herself with her food for a while, but then loses interest and energy. She puts on some music and finds herself, of all shameful things, daydreaming about sex. She remembers how thrilling it used to be to see her husband standing naked before her, how wonderfully visual a man's body is; it was remarkable, really, that something like desire, a private emotion as unseen as the wind, was translated into the physical. Until she had started working at the sleep clinic, Anna had never seen a naked man other than her husband. She was shocked at how little some of them were. She smiles, remembering the first time she did the test for nocturnal tumescence. The idea was to awaken the man and ask approximately what percentage did that represent of full arousal—usually the answer was eighty or ninety per cent, though some men, especially young ones, lied and said something comical like thirty or forty. But that first time, Anna had asked the question and looked down, said, while the man was sleepily gathering his thoughts, "What would you say, about fifty per cent?"

Luckily, he had a sense of humor. "That's pretty much our show," he said.

Anna pours a brandy and drinks it quickly, trying to quiet her nervousness for Miriam. The M.C. comes on and announces the competition, lists the names of the comedians. Miriam is the third to appear and the only woman.

Anna has a second brandy, then a third, and finally feels herself relax. She even laughs a little at some of the jokes—now from a young black man joking about his poverty while growing up in the ghetto.

The host, a slick-looking man in his fifties, announces a "very funny young woman from Pittsburgh," and then Miriam appears. Anna feels her heart clench with pride and fear. Miriam looks stylish and beautiful, relaxed in a way she never was in life. She had on more than her usual makeup, and a loose dress with tights and flat shoes that made her look younger than her twenty-six years.

"I'm from Pennsylvania," Miriam is saying, to some scattered applause in the audience. "Yeah, thanks," she says, rolling her eyes. "Not! From a section in Pittsburgh called Squirrel Hill, which, as you might have guessed, is the Jewish neighborhood. And like any good JAP, I was raised to know two things: shopping and shame." Anna laughs uneasily—Miriam was never a princess; they'd always been poor as church mice.

". . . Jews flaunt tragedy the way the goyim flaunt boats and cars. You could tell me your house just burned down, your children axe-murdered the day after your vasectomy, and what would a good Jew say? 'Shame. But sit down here on my horsehair sofa while I read to you from the diary of my grandmother, thrown from the train on her way to Auschwitz, by the light of this lamp made of Grandma Goldie's skin the day after she had too many pimientos and broke out in that unfortunate rash . . .'"

There is a ripple of laughter in the audience. Anna is stunned. Her own mother's name was Goldie, and she did die in the camps. This was information Miriam knew from the somber reverence of the seder, of Passovers. How could she take the solemn privacy of something like this and turn it into a mockery?

". . . it's true. Growing up my mother and I would do our Saturday cleaning, and instead of dusting the lampshades like everyone else, she'd hand me a jar of Nivea. And you know how your dad always says, 'When I was your age, I had to walk six miles to school in cardboard shoes after a breakfast of snow'? Well, my mother's idea of teaching me a lesson was to make me remove all valuables before entering the bathroom, then go down to the basement and turn off the water pressure for the shower. I swear, I thought for sure she was going to gas me."

The audience, to Anna's astonishment, is laughing at this.

"Mother, I'm dying in here, I can't breathe! 'So, you're dying,' she'd say. 'Make sure to use some baby oil. Another daughter I can have for free, but do you know what lampshades are going for these days? You're going to be terrific on my end table.'"

She is drunk when she arrives at the hospital, has been driving around the city for over an hour trying to figure out what to do with herself, who to turn to. But there was no one whom she could visit, no one who would understand the gravity and violation of something like this.

She goes into Albert's room after telling the clinician on duty—thankfully Anna has never seen him before—that Albert is her patient and she needs a confidential interview with him.

He seems surprised to see her, and she knows even in the shadowy light her face holds the news.

"I am officially diagnosed as an atypical somnambulist. Mild sedatives are prescribed," he says. "Come and sit," he says, patting the bed beside him. "Why are you here?"

"I do not know."

"You have been drinking?"

She nods. "But I'm glad you are feeling better."

"Anna, my beauty, my lovely rose of spring, you are troubled? Please, unload on me."

But she doesn't say anything, just sits there and studies his face, shame at war with desire. There is such a thing as cellular memory, and Anna thinks what a marvel it is really, that if she reached out to touch his hand, he would not draw away despite the pain that is, for instance, etched in the memory of the skin. Maybe faith, too, begins so small, in the interstices of cells.

"Anna?"

"Tell me a story. Tell me what you were like at twenty."

His voice seems to get younger as he talks, and she lets herself relax, soothed by a gentleness in his tone, something that goes beyond the words themselves. A playful urgency, like the young voice calling to his friend outside her window that day. Or that young man years ago, framed in the doorway of an empty classroom: she recalls his face now. A beautiful face that broke her heart because she couldn't remember ever being young enough to have such a youthful companion, because her husband had just died, and her daughter was trying to. And she kissed him as though he was at once something not real and something that could save her.

This is it now: the tender reedy green of Albert's voice, the unnamable longing she'd felt—feels—not really for a man or her own wrecked youth or even, particularly, for a respite in her loneliness, but for something quite like this, something heavy and immovable now lifting as her lips find his in the dark, drunk with desire and the wild delirium of grief.

The Mathematics
of Pendulums

Since my father died ten months ago, my six-year-old brother Jimmy has been eating dirt. Potting soil, mostly, but at times the garden variety as well.

I watch now as he roots around in the Swedish ivy on the end table and shakes a fistful of dirt in his mouth exactly like he's eating Pixie sticks. Throwing the plants away doesn't help; Jimmy just fishes them out of the garbage, even the ones I take outside.

Last week I said, "Do you want to live to see ten? Do you know the average lifespan of an earthworm? Eleven months." I made that up, but Jimmy took me seriously and made a will. He left me his entire library of Dr. Seuss and the Candyland game.

My mother took Jimmy to a child psychologist when we lived in

New York, but since we moved to Pittsburgh, she seems to have forgotten there's earth everywhere you go. She works a lot. Her new job is as an illustrations editor for children's books. Between her work and her new boyfriend, we almost never see her. Jimmy and I hate the boyfriend, Jason. He spends the night a lot and wears shoes that slip on instead of lace. One of the last bits of advice my father gave me was just this: "Beau, honey, never date men who wear slip-on shoes. It's a sure sign they're lazy." For no reason I could figure, my father started calling me by my middle name shortly before he died. I am named Amy Beau after my father's mother and the bottle of beaujolais that led to my conception one reckless night seventeen long years ago. My father is dead, as I have already mentioned.

It is freezing here in Pittsburgh. It has been snowing for a solid week, though not enough to cancel school. Christmas is a month away.

I watch from the living room window as Matty, the caretaker for our building, shovels the sidewalk. I met Matty, whose whole name is Matuso Kobayashi, a few days after we moved in. He was trimming the hedges in front of the building and I was sitting nearby watching. His apartment is on the first floor, just off the entrance. I visit quite a bit, once a day at least. I can't stand to sit around the TV watching stupid sitcoms that I can't laugh at, or listen to the radio talk shows my mother blares all evening in the kitchen and pretend that faulty wiring repair or how Jesus saves is too engrossing to be interrupted.

Matty clears the walkway to the front door, dumping the snow in two even mounds on either side of the path.

"Beau, you want me to tell you why the Chinese have slanted eyes?" Jimmy asks, putting his hands on my shoulders and kneeling on the window seat to look out.

"Beat it, beetle-breath," I say.

"The Chinese have slanted eyes because when they were little, their mothers made their pigtails too tight." He pulls at the skin and hair at his temples, narrowing his eyes into slits.

"Matty is Japanese. The Japanese have slanted eyes from squinting in disgust at six-year-old American boys with dirt under their fingernails."

Jimmy puts his hands in his pockets and turns.

"I was just kidding," I say, but he is already walking towards his bedroom. I hate myself when I'm mean to him like this. I don't know why I do it. But a year ago he would have fought back. Would have put a rubber lizard in my bed or ambushed me with a squirt gun from around every corner.

Keys rattle outside the door and then Mother appears. She dumps a stack of papers on the table she uses for a desk. "Did you start dinner?" she says.

"No."

"No. How considerate. It's not like I work ten hours a day or anything. Where's Jimmy?"

"In his room. Doing okay."

She slumps onto the couch without taking off her coat. "Do me a favor please and fix me a drink. We'll order a pizza."

I pour a double whiskey over ice and sit beside her. "How was work?"

"Busy. How was school?"

"Boring. I thought maybe we could rent videos tonight."

"That sounds good. Maybe sometime this weekend. Jason is coming over tonight."

"He's been here three times this week already. I know he spends the night. I accidentally walked in on him in the bathroom one morning. Did he tell you that?"

"Yes."

"I don't think it's very good for Jimmy to see a strange man in his Daddy's bed. I think you're mean and selfish."

I wait for the inevitable don't you dare talk to me like that speech, but her expression is blank, like she hasn't heard me at all. She pours herself another drink and says finally, "Order the pizza, why don't you. After dinner I want you to get started on those dishes. They've been sitting in the sink for a week."

Jimmy walks into the kitchen while I'm cleaning up. In the living room, I hear Mother talking in a low voice to Jason—whose cologne I can smell all the way in here—and laughing in a way that I've never heard before. She sounds like one of the girls in my class.

"Hi, Beau," Jimmy says, climbing up on the counter.

"Hi, Buddy. How's tricks?"

"Okay. I just came to see what you're doing."

"I'm having the time of my life and you're sitting in a puddle of water."

He touches the counter beneath him and shrugs.

"What's going on in the living room?"

"That man is here."

"I know." I wipe the table and turn off the sink light. "I'm just about done here. How about a game of Candyland?"

"I don't feel like it."

"I'll watch TV with you. We can watch it in the bedroom. It's almost time for 'Top Cops.'"

"Okay. I'll be in. I need some lemonade first."

I pretend to leave, but watch him from around the side of the refrigerator. He reaches behind the curtain and pulls out the African violet where I hid it. He starts with just a little, tiny crumbs he puts carefully on his tongue, then rakes the dirt deeper like he's looking for something. He touches the exposed roots of the plant then pulls off and eats a clump of soil the size of a quarter. He wrinkles his nose and begins to cry softly, looking hungry and desperate. Like he wants more than anything for the bitterness to turn sweet inside him.

I walk into the living room and over to where Mother is standing with Jason showing him her latest work. She's been obsessed with the cover of this particular book. It shows an aardvark in a field of flowers. The entire thing is done in shades of purple. The title is *Dozens of Cousins* and has baby aardvarks peeking out of the O's. Sappy things like this make me want to puke—I've no heart really.

Jason glances up at me. "Hi, Beau," he says.

"The name is Amy to you, sir. Mother, your son needs you. He is eating earth."

She sighs and goes in to get Jimmy, who is really crying and carrying on now. She struggles him into the bathroom. Jason looks at me like I've been eating dirt, too, like he's afraid I'm going to offer him a Hostess Mud Pie and he won't be able to say no because he wants to Be My Friend.

"Jeez. What's going on in there?" he says with a nervous laugh. Jimmy is screaming at the top of his voice.

I shrug. "Welcome to the Alfred Hitchcock hour."

That night I sleep like hell. Jimmy cries on and off for hours, but it's when he's quiet that I wake up and check on him. All that dirt could mess up a person. What if he gets some disease? I worry he'll suffocate from it. I know he's not breathing it in or anything, but still, I have these pictures in my head of all that dirt creeping up from his stomach and pressing on his lungs, like he will be buried alive from the inside out. Once when he was crying the loudest I went into his room to ask if he wanted to sleep with me, but he wasn't even awake. It was pathetic. A kid sobbing in his sleep like that. I wanted to slap him awake. But I just sat there for a while and let my hand be crushed in a vice grip.

Early the next morning I hear someone throwing up in the bathroom. I know it's probably Jimmy, but for a few moments I have this terrible feeling that it's my mother with morning sickness. This would be the worst thing that could happen to us. I doubt the kid would be normal. Mother is in her forties so the baby would probably be retarded and then it would have to live in a home and my mother would have to work two jobs to make ends meet—abnormal kids are expensive—and would have a heart attack from all the strain or get cancer. My father was a doctor, I know about these things. Worry too much, and before you know it you're looking at a melanoma.

I knock on the bathroom door then walk in. Jimmy is sitting on the edge of the tub staring into space.

"Are you okay? I heard you throwing up in here." His hair is stuck to his forehead and his pajama top is damp. "Jimmy?" I wave my hand in front of his eyes.

"Daddy's home," he says, looking at me for the first time. "Daddy's back. I heard him in there with Mommy."

"That's Jason, baby."

"I heard Daddy's voice."

"That wasn't Daddy. You know it wasn't Daddy."

Jimmy gets this look on his face like he had when we took him to the funeral home to see my father. My mother explained to him that Daddy would look just like he was sleeping, except he couldn't wake up. But the first thing Jimmy did was to rush up to the casket and shake him. "Daddy! Hi, Daddy!" he said. And then he just stood there staring at him, putting his G.I. Joe men in my father's hand, having little pretend battles on his chest like he expected my father to be annoyed enough to turn over and say, "Okay, enough now. Knock it off, will you?" To tell you the truth, I kind of expected it myself. I helped Jimmy sneak his Etch-a-Sketch into the casket. Jimmy was worried that Daddy would get bored. Sometimes when I want to believe in magic or God, I imagine that if I bought another Etch-a-Sketch I could use it like a Ouija board. I'd light candles and concentrate until the little knobs turned on their own and my father's handwriting appeared on the screen: "Having a great time. Wish you were here."

"How long do people stay dead, Beau?" Jimmy says now.

"Forever," I say.

"How long is forever?"

I think a minute. "As long as Christmas Eve. As long as a million Christmas Eves."

He nods and looks like he's going to be sick again.

"It's time for cartoons," I say.

"Okay. I'll be out in a minute. I need to take care of some things first." His eyes look like they belong to an old man.

I open Mother's bedroom door. The venetian blinds are pulled against the sun and cast horizontal shadows across her face. She is breathing deeply. She usually takes about a thousand valiums to help her sleep and it really puts her under; the world could fall away and she wouldn't know it. Jason is curled behind her and has one arm draped across her waist. Something about his arm like that makes me crazy. Like he thinks in her bed is exactly where he belongs. I pick up one of his stupid-looking penny loafers and throw it hard against the wall above the bed. It lands on Jason's pillow. "What the hell—" he says, sitting up.

"Mother, I hate to wake you. But your son needs you. He's been vomiting for the past four hours." She opens one bloodshot eye and squints. Her face looks bloated and lined. "I'll be right with him," she mumbles.

I go downstairs and knock on Matty's door.

"Who, please?"

"Me, please. The pest from upstairs." He opens the door. "Amy-Beau." He smiles. "Up early today. Do come in."

Matty's apartment is done in warm shades of coral and cream. It always smells so good in here, too, like flowers or exotic spices. Once, Matty took out the trunk that held his wife's things, let me try on the old kimonos that had been in his wife's family for three generations. I wore one all afternoon liking the feel of the cool satin against my skin. The kimono and her silk scarves smelled just like the air in Matty's rooms, but instead of giving me the creeps it made me feel close to her. Like I could feel her next to me, friendly and curious, as Matty showed me the love letters she had written to him while they were dating. There were hundreds of them, but the most amazing thing was none of the paper had turned yellow and the ink had hardly faded. I can't read Japanese, of course, but I can recognize the character for love—which in Japanese is written more than one way, depending on which kind. Married love is two stick figures in a pagoda. The character that stands for love in families has so many lines and is so intricate that one tiny mistake ruins the entire thing. If your hand slipped while drawing it or something, you'd have to cross the whole thing out and start over. Anytime you see something that looks like a blot or smudge in Japanese writing, it's a bad thing. It means shame or losing honor.

Matty and I sit at the kitchen table and he pours me some tea. His hand brushes against mine and it feels warm and smooth. "How is the mother and the brother?" he says.

"They're fine," I say.

"Yes? Fine?"

"I want to ask you something. If you saw someone eating weird things like dirt, what would you think?"

He thinks a minute then says, "I would think the individual suffered an imbalance."

"Like not getting a balanced diet you mean?"

"Perhaps a physical imbalance, yes. But also perhaps like alcoholics. It is not the whiskey or beer that one craves, but the high. Maybe an individual who eats dirt does not crave the earth, but its gravity."

I look away from him, watch the snow fall outside, collecting on the seats of the swing set in the backyard. The heat in this apartment feels like it's been turned up about a million degrees. I feel little beads of sweat at my eyebrows. So much can go wrong. Like I might say, Jimmy eats dirt, not just crumbs either. And Matty might call my mother who might call people to take Jimmy away. They might lock him up for the rest of his life. I've thought about what I would do if that happened. I would burn down a car wash and say I was on a mission from God then have myself locked up in the room next to his.

"Amy-Beau." I look over at him and he smiles. "Have you had any dreams?"

I nod. Matty takes this seriously. He says not trying to figure out your dreams is like not opening a letter.

"One night I dreamed that my father was standing on a bridge. He was throwing baby chicks in test tubes over the side."

"Yes?" Matty says, putting bagels on the table—cream cheese on his, apricot jam and peanut butter on mine.

"One test tube landed in a pile of mud and the chick crawled out. One hit the cement and the chick died."

Matty dunks the end of his bagel into his tea. I love it when he does this—it reminds me of my Italian grandfather who used to put hunks of bread in a bowl of coffee so it looked like soup.

"Father has been deceased a year?"

"Almost a year, yes."

"After my wife died, I dreamed with her every night for two years. Right now I dream with my brother. He is right now suffering from cancer to the throat. You were how old when the father died?"

"Sixteen."

"Sixteen. You had the father for sixteen years, the brother only six."

"And the mother had the father too long," I say, remembering her impatience with him at the end. He stopped eating and sleeping and became obsessed with buying animation cels from Disney movies. In my closet, I have an actual production cel of "The Little Mermaid." The last birthday gift he gave me.

"Did father have illness?"

I knew he'd get around to asking this eventually. "No, Matty, Father did not have illness. He offed himself."

He frowns. "Offered self?"

"No, offed himself. You know." I make a gun out of my thumb and forefinger and hold it to my head.

"Oh," he says, and looks away.

"We got on his nerves a lot," I say. "Jimmy was a big slob who never picked up his toys. I complained about everything all the time.

We drove my father crazy. I got three C's on my report card that semester and once I told him I hated him."

Matty waves this away. "Not the fault of you or the brother. The father had personal unhappiness." He pats my hand. "Yes? Okay?"

"Yes. Okay."

My father was tired of living, that's all I know: "So damn tired of buttoning and unbuttoning," was all his note said. I sort of know the feeling.

"You come back later and bring the brother," Matty says now.

At first I think they're playing a trick on me. Hiding, ready to spring out from behind the shower curtain, grab my ankle from under the bed. But ours is a tiny apartment and it takes me five minutes to search every inch. Jimmy and my mother are gone. The TV is blaring, Jimmy's bowl of cereal is on the coffee table, and my mother's purse is hanging behind the closet door. "Okay. Very funny. You can come out now," I yell, but I already know they're not here.

Jimmy's pajamas are in a heap on the bathroom floor and my heart slows down a little: kidnappers wouldn't wait for him to change his clothes. I search the floor anyway for signs of evidence. I don't know what kind, but this is what you're supposed to do.

On the edge of the bathtub are my father's shaving mug and brush. The bristles are wet. I can smell, too, faint traces of his aftershave on it and I can't tell you what this does to me.

The longer I'm alone, the more convinced I am that something happened. Jason could be a killer. Or somebody could have just walked in here and forced them out at gunpoint. I should call the police, I should run down and tell Matty they're missing. But instead I crawl into my closet, hide beneath the blankets and sweaters.

If I have to, drowning is the method I'll choose. Supposedly only the drowning can see Christ. Anyway, I am not afraid to die, it's being alive I find terrifying.

I don't know how long I'm in the closet, but the next thing I know my mother is calling me. Her voice sounds far away and makes the hair on the back of my neck stand up, bristly, like my father's shaving brush. I don't move until I hear other, familiar, sounds: the TV channels being changed, the thud of keys on the desk.

"There you are," she says when I walk into the living room. She smooths down my hair. "Were you napping?" She touches my forehead. "Are you sick?"

"Where the hell have you been?"

Jimmy turns around from the TV to look at me. "I heard that. You swore, you used a swear word."

"Excuse me?" my mother says.

"Where have you been?"

"That's better. Didn't you—"

"I come back up here, everybody's gone, what am I supposed to think?"

She looks down at the coffee table, moves the cereal bowl. "Jimmy, for crying out loud, why did you put your bowl on top of it?" She hands me the note: "Went to get Christmas tree. Be back in couple of hours."

"I didn't do it on purpose!" Jimmy says. "I didn't do it on purpose." He starts crying.

"I hate notes. Next time call. Next time come and tell me where you're going. Just don't leave me a note."

"You know something? I am more than a little sick of the way you talk to me lately."

"All I said—"

"It's not what you said. It's the way you said it."

"Here comes Santa!" Jason says from the doorway, struggling with the tree. He looks at us from underneath it: Jimmy crying facedown on the couch. My mother and I scowling.

"Hey now, how about some holiday cheer?" Jason says.

"How about a holiday assassin?" I say.

"I hate Christmas," Jimmy says.

"Just put the tree down anywhere," Mother says.

Because the bathroom has the only door that locks, this is where I go. I want to decorate the tree about as much as I want to walk barefoot in the snow. I take my books in with me; it's been weeks since I studied and I have four Shakespeare plays to read for English class—the only course I'm not failing—and I'm about two natural disasters behind in Geology; we're on tidal waves now, but I still don't

The Mathematics of Pendulums 105

understand what makes the earth quake and I couldn't tell you the difference between a fault and a reverse fault.

"Beau," Jimmy says at the keyhole. "Please come out. I'll put the eunuchs on." This is our name for the monks who sing Gregorian chants and it's a kind of tradition to listen to them while we decorate the tree.

"No eunuchs this year, baby. Why don't you play Alice in Chains?"

His footsteps pound away and I open my algebra book. I used to have all A's in Math, but in the past year a simple thing like solving for unknown x's and y's makes me feel like I'm about to break out in a rash.

"Amy." My mother taps on the door. "We're decorating the tree."

"Okay." She doesn't move away. "Okay," I say again.

"What are you doing in there?"

"Just sitting here passing through nature into eternity, Mother." My favorite Shakespeare line.

"What's that supposed to mean?"

"I don't think I can help with the tree. I have all this homework."

"Make the time. Make the effort and get out here."

"I cannot heave my heart into my hand." Shakespeare was the original smartass. He must have driven his own mother bonkers.

"Open this door. Open this door right now."

"Where's Daddy's shaving brush? It was here this morning."

"I don't know."

"You're lying. You gave it to Jason, didn't you? Or did you throw it away?"

"If you're not out here in five minutes there's going to be trouble. I'll take this door off the hinges if I have to."

But of course she doesn't. I sit here for over an hour and nothing happens. I'm almost not real. But then Jimmy is crying at the keyhole begging me to let him in saying they won't use the angel, that Jason bought a new star for the tree top and the angel we have used every Christmas is being retired because her wings are bent. I let Jimmy in.

"Please stop crying," I say.

"Daddy is dead. My Daddy is dead."

My heart feels like it will stop beating when he says this. "Daddy's not dead. He's in Belgium."

Jimmy looks at me. "What's that?"

"It's a country. It's where you can go if heaven seems too far away. It's like heaven only better. You don't have to go to church and you eat chocolate for every meal." I don't know why I'm lying to the kid like this. Why I'm saying these things. But I sound so convincing that I almost believe it myself. "People in Belgium are nice. All the parents are happy and love each other forever. All the children do well in school and never complain about anything. Everybody loves everybody so much that nothing bad ever happens. They play Candyland and Pin the Tail on the Donkey and nobody litters."

"How long do people stay there?"

"Forever, Jimmy. I keep telling you forever. If you were Daddy, would you want to come back?"

"Maybe he'll miss us. Maybe he'll visit us."

"He doesn't remember us. They put something in the chocolate to make you forget." I hold a wad of toilet paper in front of his nose: "Blow," I say. "Do you know what will happen if you keep crying all the time?"

"What?" he says.

"You'll never have to pee again."

He looks shocked and stops crying immediately. "Is it my bedtime yet?" he says finally.

"Your bedtime has come and gone. But I want to give you mine."

He smiles a little at our old joke. "No, my dear, I couldn't take yours. I have never taken a bedtime from a lady."

"Darling, I insist. If you don't take it, I'll just give it to Goodwill with your old suits."

I run a bath for him and get out a fresh pair of flannel pajamas. I put them on the bench in front of the space heater so they'll be warm. "Sweet dreams, Jimmy."

"Sweeter to you," he says.

The tree looks vomitous. The star on top is the cheapest-looking piece of shit I've ever seen. Even the ornaments are new. They are all the same, red and satiny, and the lights around them are all white and don't blink. And for the first time my mother has had her way with the tinsel: it is carefully draped on every branch. My parents fought about this every year. Last Christmas my father whispered to me: "Your mother's taste and judgment are impeccable. But she's misguided when it comes to tinsel. Tinsel-tossing is like abstract art; it should never look as if it's been arranged. Never drape, always toss. Think of Jackson Pollock and let it fly from the shoulder."

My mother notices me standing in the doorway and looks at me like she dares me to say anything.

"Hi, Amy. How's the homework?" Jason says.

"Fine. I'm finally understanding earthquakes."

"That's good," Jason says.

I stare at that terrible tree without all our traditional ornaments, the ones Jimmy and I made in school, the antique ones that had been in my father's family for years, and I am sick. I say, "You want me to tell you the difference between a fault and a reverse fault?"

"Excuse me?" my mother says.

"Nothing. I'll be back," I say, walking to the door.

"No. It's too late to be bothering that poor old man. Amy!"

I slam the door and run downstairs.

Matty takes a long time to answer my knock.

"Did I wake you?"

"Yes. But all right."

"It's too noisy to go to sleep upstairs and I was wondering if I could stay here."

"Certainly," he says. "Always welcome, my young friend."

Something about the way he says this makes me ashamed that I'm not a better person; when people are nice to me like this I could cry I'm so grateful.

Matty turns a lamp on and fixes up the sofa for me. The sheets are peach and embroidered with tiny flowers. "This linen, I never have opportunities to use. They were the bedsheets of my daughter, made by my wife. For the bridal dowry, which has come to nothing."

"I didn't know you had a daughter."

He laughs. "She, too, does not know. Yes. She studies the stars in Texas." He stretches the sheets tight and arranges the pillows. "Does the mother know you're here?"

"Yes."

He looks down at me and smiles. "A good night, Amy-Beau."

"A good night to you."

But I cannot sleep. I get a glass of milk and sit in the dark by the window. I count the cars that pass outside. The headlights flicker along the walls and I imagine that they're angels, already there in the dark waiting for a car to come along and push them out of hiding. Sometimes I want to believe there are such things as this, or that heaven is just another country like I told Jimmy. But like my father, I've no faith, really; anytime I try to imagine God I see Wayne Newton. My father once said yes, he believed in God, but that wasn't the same as faith was it, and respect was a different matter entirely. My father was a pediatric oncologist, a cancer doctor for kids, and he saw children die all the time. God, he said, was the original Mr. Las Vegas, up there at the crap tables throwing dice.

I stand in the doorway of Matty's bedroom.

He turns to look at me. "Yes?"

"Where do people go after they die? How long is forever?"

He sighs. "I have no answer for that, Amy-Beau."

"Why?" I'm a little shocked; Matty has an answer for everything.

"You must find your own beliefs."

"I can't sleep. What if I'm never able to sleep again? I'm afraid to go to sleep."

"Nothing to fear. Sleep is just a different kind of awake," he says. He gets up and lights a cigarette. "Come in. Come here," he says. He folds down the bedcovers. I slip in. He sits in the chair beside me. "One can bring on sleep. I had to learn. After my wife dies, I am lonesome as an onion peddler at the nighttime. Close your eyes, and now imagine you are in a pool of warm water. Imagine the blue sky above. Now colors against blue. Imagine a salmon, bright pink to fill the blue, and starting now to flake. All the pieces turn into red balloons carrying you up and up. Now you fly over storms in Africa."

I close my eyes and try it, but I've no imagination, really, I am only ever myself. "Do you believe in God?" I whisper.

"Do not ask," he says. "Concentrate. Now this: begin naming objects."

"Objects?"

"Anything at all. Not fitting together. I will start listing: Bookends, giraffes, thumbtacks, carpet slippers, a beating heart, an egg turner . . ."

I name a few silently: windows, saxophones, fenders, Malamutes . . . and what happens is, the more I name, the more things pop into my head on their own.

I begin to relax.

"This," Matty whispers, "is how Mr. Isaac Newton proved to himself the presence of a divinity. All objects obey the laws of gravity. All suspended objects obey the same mathematical principles, regardless of weight or density. A pendulum of any size will always in every case swing back. No exceptions. Everything is obeying existing order and pattern."

"This wouldn't make me believe in God, though," I say.

"No, nor I. But faith, I believe, obeys the law of suspended objects. Faith in what one touches or loves or remembers generates momentum such as Mr. Newton's pendulums. What we set in motion always is coming back."

That night I sleep better than I have in weeks. I am alone in the bedroom when I wake up. The clock reads seven-thirty. I find Matty in the kitchen fixing bagels and coffee.

"Good morning," Matty says. "How was your sleep and dreams?"

"Good," I say. "No dreams."

"The mother called, asking me to tell you she must go shopping for Christmas. You are to babysit."

"What time?"

"As soon as breakfast is had."

I do all of Matty's dishes and rinse my hands and face in cold water so that going upstairs will be less of a shock; the heat in our apartment has never worked right. I borrow one of Matty's sweaters then go upstairs.

I find Jimmy in my mother's bed. He looks bad. His face is pale and he looks like he's aged about ten years since I last saw him. It's his eyes, maybe: he just stares ahead like he expects nothing to be there. Before, he'd look all around a room like there might be a surprise party about to happen with people jumping out of closets and from behind furniture.

He seems to be aware of me only when I sit on the bed. He looks pathetically small buried in all those blankets. Sometimes when Jimmy is watching TV or something, I want to rig up a seat belt and shoulder strap for him on the sofa; the kid always seems to be on the verge of a collision.

"Why are you still in bed?"

"I am sick today."

"Sick where?"

"My stomach and my heart."

"Your heart?"

He doesn't answer and I try to joke around with him, yank the covers off, put my cold hands on his back. He flinches away. "Can I get you anything? Soup? Oatmeal? Swedish ivy?" He won't laugh, won't even look at me. "Have you been eating dirt again?"

"Yes."

"Why?"

"I don't know why."

I go into the kitchen and look up the number of a mental health clinic. My hands are shaking, and the woman on the other end has to say "hello" twice before I can speak. "My brother eats dirt," I say. "But he's not crazy or violent or anything." After making her promise that they won't lock him up in the psycho ward, I set up an appointment for next Wednesday.

I find some bouillon cubes and a jar of cocktail onions and go back to Jimmy. "We're going to get you fixed up, okay? We'll get you on the wagon. I brought some snacks. Have a grisly." This is Jimmy's name for bouillon cubes, something he has loved since he was tiny. He sucks on them like breath mints.

"I'm so cold," he says. "I feel so cold."

I take off my shoes and get into bed with him. "Move in close to me. I'm a furnace." He puts his feet under mine and even through my thick socks I can feel how cold they are. His toes curl around my ankles like little fists. I hold him tight against the length of me.

The next thing I know it's late afternoon. The bottom half of the window is steamed and the light above it is dusky pink. There is a cold draft of air from somewhere and just for a moment I want to imagine that my father has bent over us as we slept and it is his breath I see fogged on the glass. I remember the top part of the street sign my father stole for me shortly before he died: "Amy Drive," it read, but for some reason he'd inserted a comma between the words so it's become something of a command. I think of all the details I can about him: the way he looked in his white coat. The last pair of shoes he bought. The strong smell of aftershave and Listerine in the morning. But I feel nothing.

A little later, I hear my mother come in, hear the rustle of packages and bags. Even without peeking at them as I usually would, I know the gifts are probably all wrong. I doubt my mother has noticed that my size has changed or that Jimmy no longer plays with toys.

I watch the numbers change on the clock. Five minutes pass, then ten, and she still hasn't come to check on us. We could be axe-murdered in here. We could have choked to death or gotten into her valiums and died in our sleep.

I find her in the bathroom sitting on the edge of the tub. She is still wearing her coat and one glove. One shoe is off, the other dangles from the tips of her toes.

"Mother," I say softly.

"Yes."

"What are you doing?"

She doesn't answer, and her face is as white as Jimmy's.

I say, "Attention all units. We have a two-eleven in progress. Perpetrator is armed and dangerous."

She looks up finally. "Come and sit beside me. Come and sit with me for awhile." I can smell a bunch of different perfumes on her, like she spent some time testing fragrances at the Clinique counter.

"I saw a man in front of Kaufmann's who looked so much like your father that I followed him for three blocks. He even had that thing with his shoulder. You know, the way your father carried one shoulder higher than the other."

"It wasn't him, though. It couldn't have been him, right?"

It takes me a minute to realize she's crying. I have never seen this, and I want to get out of here, out of the bathroom, out of Pittsburgh, out of the country, even. But I stay where I am and ask again: "It couldn't have been him, could it? There's no way. It was just someone who looked like him." I want suddenly to go outside and eat a handful or two of snow. Bury myself under every blanket in the house. Sit in front of the TV and watch every stupid movie that comes on. I think about how long my life seems, about my brother's ruined stomach and my mother's nervous boyfriend. I think about how my father always closed his eyes when he shaved in the mornings, his chin angling up to meet the blade, his expression calm and peaceful under the practiced motion of his hand. I think of the tinsel dangling in glittered order on the tree, and of all the stars in Texas.

Tall Pittsburgh

At my father's insistence, I'd just completed charm
school at Sears. Every Saturday for six weeks, I'd trudge past the
boys' department and home appliances to the back of the store where
for three hours I'd submit to the dubious counsel of Mrs. Moynihan,
a hefty-hipped matron of fifty with a crepey neck and lower legs like
inverted bowling pins.

There were eight other girls besides me, all around my own age
but much smaller: at fourteen, I'd reached my full height of five feet
nine inches, and was the huge and hulking bear at the table of di-
minutive Goldilockses.

Mrs. Moynihan couldn't figure my purpose in her class any more
than I could—most of the other students wanted to be in beauty

pageants or be the perfect prom date—and we were mutually contemptuous of each other: I offended her aesthetic of feminine allure, and she just simply offended me. I was no junior, no little ruffled petite, with a ceiling of perfectly coifed hair over a boy-crazy brain.

I suppose guilt got the best of her—my father paid her good money, after all—and toward the end of the course she made me stay after class for remedial fashion lessons. I tried on garments from Sears Tall Shop, horrible polyester career clothing for suburban housewives who worked part-time. She looked on with disapproval as I tugged at the sleeves or fussed with the hemlines, as though my height were a result of bad judgment on my part, something I had willed on myself.

"Is your mother deceased, dear?" she said to me one Saturday.

"Uh-huh."

She nodded. "I thought so."

"Why?"

"Your blues."

"My blues?"

"The aqua slacks and the powder blue blouse. That's usually a father's choice."

What did she think, that my father still dressed me? I'd worn these shades together forever and no one ever told me they clashed.

But I was a good sport about the charm school, just as I had been about the ballet classes and majorette camp, the piano lessons and modeling courses—all things my father signed me up for without my consent. I was accustomed to coming down to breakfast and finding the course booklet from the community center next to my plate. Inside, circled in red, would be the courses he'd enrolled me in for the upcoming quarter. It made him happy to have me in these classes, and he didn't seem to notice or care that the things I studied had no appreciable effect on me: I was still as clumsy as ever after learning ballet and ice-skating; every garment I attempted to sew was left unfinished because I couldn't get the zipper right. He didn't even mind that I broke the same window twice learning to toss that damn baton.

I assumed that after charm school ended I would be free until fall. I was looking forward to hanging out at the mall and swimming pool with my friends. It had been a particularly grueling six months as far as the extracurricular activities were concerned: I'd taken ballet and modern dance; figure-skating; water gymnastics; singing, guitar, and piano lessons; cake-decorating; quilting; flower arranging; Oriental watercolors; and the Art of Conversation.

But even at fourteen I could be philosophical about it, figuring that my father worked hard to give me things, that he loved me completely, all the way down to the depths of his wild, chaotic heart. Besides, the ten-year anniversary of my mother's death was approaching, and other than the restaurants he owned and his antique cars, I was all he had.

One afternoon I came home from the pool and found my father upstairs, in what had been my mother's dressing room. It had two huge walk-in closets, three enormous chiffoniers, and a vanity table still covered with her cosmetics and perfumes. The door to one of the closets was open, and I heard the rustling of dry-cleaning bags.

"Dad?" I called.

"Come on in here, Gina," he said.

"What are you doing?" I went in, sat on the edge of the sofa. The room smelled of mothballs and, faintly, of perfume.

I looked around—I rarely came in here, and certainly never made myself comfortable. The lace curtains had yellowed and the blinds at all the windows were pulled. Adjoining this room was the bedroom my parents had shared and where my father still slept. The bed was huge, "big enough for a whole East German family," as my exchange student friend Judith said when I gave her a tour of the house. The head and foot boards were antique, rosewood carved with angels and chunky little cherubs. The bed was so high you needed to climb two steps to get into it. I remembered being in this bed as a child, crawling in between my parents after a nightmare or on Sunday mornings. I was four when my mother died, but remembered little about her.

My father emerged from the closet holding two evening gowns. "This is a Halston," he said, holding up a red and gold sequined number with a scalloped, deeply scooped neckline. "This might be too wintery," he said, draping it over the back of a chair. "I have a special affection for that dress. Your mother had that on when she told me she was pregnant. We were going to a Christmas party. *You* were behind all those sequins." He looked up at me and smiled. "This might be more appropriate," he said, holding up the second gown, a strapless black taffeta.

"More appropriate for what?" I said.

"Slip this on over your bathing suit."

I worked myself into the dress, knowing even before I put it on that it wouldn't fit. My mother was tiny, five feet two or three, weighing not much more than a hundred pounds. How she ever gave birth to a gigantic creature with size ten feet was a mystery to all of us.

My father tugged at the zipper, but it wouldn't budge. "Well, I guess this won't work," he said. "I thought this one might fit you. Your mother wore it at her heaviest weight. She was eight months pregnant."

"Oh gee, Dad, thanks for not making me feel like the biggest beached whale of the Western world."

"I didn't mean it that way. You're beautiful. I have a photograph of your mother at eighteen that looks just like you."

"Why, is it double-exposed?"

"Very funny."

"So why am I trying on evening gowns?"

He pulled a sheet of paper from his back pocket and handed it to me. "I've entered you in the Miss Tall Pittsburgh Beauty Pageant. These are the rules."

"Miss Tall Pittsburgh?" An image of the steel building flashed in my head: a looming, blocky girl towering over Bert Parks. Fay Wray and King Kong. Someone who would have to climb little steps like the ones beside my parents' bed to crown me. "Haven't you noticed there's one big problem?"

"What?"

"I am not beautiful."

"Says who?"

"Says everybody but you. I'm fat, Dad." I turned around and glanced at my reflection in the mirror. "My butt looks like a bag of popcorn."

"Don't worry about your weight. The pageant is in September. You can safely lose fifteen pounds by then."

"And then there's my hair."

"Gina, all you have to do is worry about what you'll perform. I'll hire people to take care of your outside."

I looked down at the contest rules. At the top was a photograph of the reigning Miss Tall Pittsburgh. She was described as five feet seven, nineteen years old, and a sophomore at Smith College majoring in English. Her interests were poetry, horseback riding, and meeting people. She wanted to be a broadcast journalist. The contest was for girls between fourteen and nineteen years of age, with a minimum height requirement of five feet seven. Contestants would be judged in the categories of swimsuit, evening gown, and talent, as well as private interviews with the judges, who would ask the contestants to discuss relevant and important current issues such as education, homelessness, etc.

"Dad, I have never said no to anything you wanted me to do. But please don't make me do this."

"Why be shy?"

"I don't want to do it."

"Did you see what the winner gets? A contract option with the Ford Agency. A ten thousand dollar college scholarship. Ten thousand! Do you know how many *fettucine con vongoli* dinners I'd have to sell to give you that kind of money for school?"

"Why do I need a scholarship? I thought we were pretty rich."

"Money doesn't grow on trees."

"I'll put myself through college. I'm not doing it."

Mrs. Anneliese De Kamp ran a school for modeling and beauty pageant hopefuls. The graduates from the De Kamp School of Beauty and Pageant Management had a remarkable success rate in regional and national competitions—everything from Dairy Princess and Rodeo Round-Up Queen to Miss Teen USA. What really impressed my father was that she offered a money-back guarantee if I didn't win or place.

"No doubt," she said, the day my father brought her home to meet me. "There's no doubt in my mind she'll take first or second." She walked around me as though I were a horse she was thinking of buying. "I divide my girls into three categories. One is All-American. Strawberry blonde, freckles, devoted to Jesus, motherhood, pie-baking. The second is the Blonde Bitch Ball-Breaker from Hell, which you are not." Mrs. De Kamp, in her tight crushed velvet short shorts and popcorn tube top, looked like she might have once competed in this division. She was maybe thirty-eight or forty, a Harlow blonde wanting to go Garbo at the roots, with bright orange lipstick and coppery eye shadow that made her look like a peach not quite picked in time. Mrs. De Kamp was a gum-chewer. "You, sugar, I would put in the third category. The Exotic Other. You, my dear, have Factor X."

"Yes," my father said. "What is that?"

"Factor X is the mysterious quality which suggests that while her looks might be exotic, Italian or Latin or African, her attitude and mannerisms are saying, I am American! I belong to 4-H and volunteer at the Red Cross! I see nothing tacky about honeymooning at Niagara Falls!"

Mrs. De Kamp waved her arms as though she were holding a giant flag. She giggled. "I am exaggerating for the point of explanation." She turned to me. "You're a beautiful young woman."

"You're hired," my father said.

"My fees are two hundred dollars a day, plus compensation for overtime."

"Money is no object," my father said. "You can start right now. I'll be at the restaurant in Squirrel Hill if anything comes up."

When my father left, I said, "If it's all the same to you, I'd rather be the ball-breaking bitch from hell."

Mrs. De Kamp cracked her gum, said, "We'll see."

Over the next few weeks, Mrs. De Kamp coached me in everything from pageant walk—step step pause, step step pause—to the things I should say to the judges in the private interviews. We disagreed over my topic: I wanted to speak about domestic violence, which puzzled her.

"By that you mean battered wives and such?"

"Exactly."

"But what do you know of that, sugar? I can't imagine your sweet-tempered father ever raising his hand against anyone, let alone his family. Am I wrong?"

"Well, no."

"Then I think you should consider a closer, more personal subject."

She picked a gown from one of the four my father had had delivered that morning from a designer boutique in Shadyside, one of Pittsburgh's swank, upscale neighborhoods. "You're very lucky, do you know? Usually it's the other way around: the girls want to enter the contests, and the parents object. I must say I've never worked with such a cooperative father." She held up a peach satin and feather dress in front of me and made sounds of approval.

"I'm allergic to feathers," I said.

She let out an exasperated sigh. "You're going to have to give me a little help, Gina. I can't win this thing for you. Your father is paying me good money to see you crowned."

"But why, is what I want to know."

She put the gown on the reject pile and picked up another. "I'm thinking over the overall package, the overall presentation. What I think we'll do is have you talk to the judges about what it's been like to grow up without a mother. Second, we'll dress you in something that is quite obviously too sophisticated for you. Big shoulder pads, slightly too big in the bust. This will hit the judges at the subconscious level. A little girl playing dress-up in Mommy's clothes. And an updated '50s style two-piece for the swimsuit competition. Have you thought about what you'd like to do for the talent?"

"I don't want to sing or dance. I thought I'd do a dramatic poetry reading."

"Interesting. What poem?"

I pointed out a page from the poetry anthology we used in sophomore English.

Mrs. De Kamp glanced at it. "'Dover Beach.' Huh. Won't work."

"Why not?"

"Too frivolous. The beach babe theme has been overdone. California girls are definitely out. I'm thinking you should sing. Your father tells me you've studied voice. He suggested 'Fly Me to the Moon.'"

Mrs. De Kamp calibrated the tension on the exercise bicycle. This was part of the general fitness program she designed for me: thirty minutes on the stationary bike in the morning, swimming the laps equivalent to a mile in the afternoon, and a twenty-minute workout with free weights in the evening. Of course I was dieting, too, and had lost ten pounds in three weeks—which I was happy about, except that I was constantly hungry and thinking about food. To help fight temptation, Mrs. De Kamp taught me to imagine that food was the enemy, that every morsel I put in my mouth was a little piece of unhappiness. "Sugar," she said, "among women, weight is the great equalizer. Put three women in a room together, one rich, one at the top of her career, and one thin. Who do you think gets attention and envious stares? Men don't get clubby with chubbies."

As I dropped weight, exercised, and spent time with my hair and makeup, I began to understand the De Kamp theory of allure: not just boys my own age, but strange men on the street began to notice me. But what I didn't get was why this was supposed to make me feel good. Even when one of the most popular boys in school asked me to meet him in a deserted classroom, his kisses, his hand inside my shirt, didn't seem to have anything to do with me. "Pretty pretty pretty" he said over and over, like it was the name of somebody else in the room.

"I have an idea," my father said one afternoon. We were in the garage where he was polishing the antique Rolls-Royce that would take me to and from the pageant. "I'm thinking you should have a stage name."

"Why?" I watched as he worked the wax into the paint on the hood, felt the reverence and hostility that all beautiful things inspire, and had a perverse impulse to spill my whole can of Diet Pepsi on the mint-condition upholstery.

"Well, you know the winner is optioned by the Ford Agency. And I've been noticing that models usually have unusual names like Elle or Jade or Liberty."

"What did you have in mind?" I said.

"I think Coco is a cute name."

"You gotta be kidding. Coco Tambellini. It sounds like the name of a stripper."

"What about Liberty?"

"Liberty Tambellini. Good, Dad. Now I sound like something that floats toward Ellis Island."

"These are just suggestions." He started to whistle. "Yes siree, one classic beauty deserves another." He patted the car and winked at me.

"Did Mom ever do this kind of thing?" I said.

He paused in his waxing but did not look up. "Beauty pageants, you mean?"

"Yeah."

"She didn't need to," he said quietly. "She was the queen of all her days."

"If she didn't do this, then why do I have to? If she were here she'd never let me do this."

"You're sure of that, are you?"

"I can't be beautiful like she was. I can't look like that."

"You're a different kind of beautiful, Gina. Your mother will be twenty-seven and beautiful forever. But you won't. Your beauty will end before your life does. That's the way it is with most people. That's the way it should be." He picked up a clean rag and went on buffing and shining. "Anna," he said quietly, as though he saw my mother somewhere beneath his hand. "Every time I looked at her I thought I would live forever. How can I describe that kind of beauty to you?"

"It's all right, you don't have to."

"In case I have to do an interview or something, you know, if the newspaper wants to interview the father of the winning contestant, I've come up with a theory of beauty." He paused. "The things of greatest beauty always affirm our belief in immortality. How, you're wondering? Because the truly beautiful is rare and alien. Why, for instance, can I sell fifty pounds of catfish if I tell people it was caught that morning? Because it's so recently from an alien world. Why do we love a beautiful woman? Because she represents the strange, the unknown. What's the greatest unknown for a human being? Death. A beautiful young woman is the symbolic death and resurrection of us all."

"Dad, please."

"Please what?"

I shook my head. "It's bad enough I don't have cleavage. Now you want me to be Christ."

My father sighed—something he picked up from Mrs. De Kamp. "Is it so wrong to love beautiful things? To want beautiful things in my life?"

I looked down at the car. In the gloomy twilight it was as stark as bone. "I just don't want you to be disappointed," I said.

"I couldn't possibly be." He looked up at me and smiled.

"You are going to talk about what it's like growing up without a mother," the head judge said as I sat down. I was wearing a Chanel suit, borrowed from the cache of clothes Mrs. De Kamp kept expressly for these occasions. It was at least ten years old—part of the overall packaging of my image—and smelled like cedar and roses. It was a lightweight gray wool and I was sweating.

"Yes," I said. "I'm nervous." Not only nervous, but ill-prepared; Mrs. De Kamp, I suppose, assumed I wouldn't have any trouble talking about something like this, but I wanted suddenly to talk about anything but this. "My mother died when I was four. Everybody says she was one of the most beautiful women in the world. I've seen her pictures, so I believe it. But I can't remember her alive. I could when I was younger, before I knew that she was this great beauty. The day she died I was in preschool. I remember we were making clay handprints. It was like everything in the room got silent for a minute. Then I heard her voice behind me. I turned, but I didn't see her. Just as I put my hand in the clay, I felt her hand covering mine, pressing down. When it dried, the print was deep, like there really had been extra pressure."

"What about now?" one of the judges said. "Do you think of her and miss her now that you're almost a woman yourself?"

"Sort of, yeah."

"In what way?"

I thought a minute. Mrs. De Kamp and I had been over and over this. I was supposed to talk about the missing role model of my mother and how my father more than made up for "my motherless state by stressing the importance of traditional values which included the timeless ideal of beauty and feminine achievement, embodied by the spirit of this pageant and others like it." I had this memorized, but I couldn't understand what it had to do with a dead mother. Plus, according to the De Kamp guidelines, I was supposed to pause after a judge asked me a question, not hesitate. The idea was to give the impression that I was gathering my thoughts, not spouting a rehearsed speech. Since I thought I was blowing it anyway, I decided just to go ahead and tell them what I really thought; no one had ever asked me before.

"Since I decided to enter this pageant I sometimes wonder what good it is to be beautiful." I went on to talk about the time I had found an envelope of things from my mother's last stay in the hospital. The cancer had started in her ovaries, and eventually spread to other parts of her body. There was an X-ray of her lungs with a gray tumor the size of a grapefruit. I stared and stared: not at the tumor, but at the outline of her breasts over it. I was glad that I was flat-chested; anytime I saw big breasts I thought of disease.

"Sometimes I worry that I won't live beyond the age of my mother. But that means half my life is over."

"Does your father talk about your mother a lot? What she was like, what kinds of things she liked to do?"

"She liked being beautiful."

"One last question, Gina," the head judge said. "If you could be someone other than who you are, who would you be?"

I hadn't expected this kind of question, and I have no idea why I said what I did. I looked the judge in the eye and said, "A poltergeist."

Because I believed I'd blown it with the judges in my interview, I was relaxed the night of the competition. I was pretty sure that once I lost my father would finally give up trying to improve me, finally see that I was not beautiful, that I had a limited voice range, and that my upper thighs in a bathing suit were like a whole set of carry-on Samsonite.

Mrs. De Kamp made me eat three grapefruits in a row that afternoon, a natural diuretic to get rid of excess water weight. Professionals from Body Goddesses came to do my hair and makeup at five o'clock. Mrs. De Kamp supervised to make sure I didn't look too vampy; up until the last I was begging her to let me be the ball-breaking bitch from hell. The makeup people, under Mrs. De Kamp's direction, played up my eyes with lots of liner, stained my lips crimson. She seemed pleased. I thought I looked like a reject from the cast of *West Side Story*.

At seven the antique Rolls delivered me to Soldiers' and Sailors' Memorial Hall, where the pageant was being held. I was shuffled into the dressing room with about fifty other girls and their mothers. Mrs. De Kamp was there with me along with one of the women from Body Goddesses to touch up my face. The other girls and their mothers stared at us. I was the only one there who brought her own makeup and wardrobe people.

The first two events were the bathing suit and evening gown competitions. I wore a sequined pink dress that was half a size too big, in keeping with the De Kamp theory of subliminal packaging, and a two-piece '50s bathing suit which gave my breasts the Jane Russell ice-cream cone look. I was more or less bored by the whole production. But then something happened when it was time for me to perform. I felt like I had been drugged, felt this eerie calm and warmth all around me. Voices seemed far away and everything looked like it was in slow, but vivid, motion.

I took the stage wearing a two-piece retro suit of gray flannel and a modified fedora. I was wearing my mother's watch and pearls. I listened for the opening bars of "Somewhere Over the Rainbow" and began to sing. Midway through my number I realized what it was that was making me feel so giddy: I wanted to win. I wanted that stupid crown, cleverly constructed to look like the Pittsburgh skyline from the vantage point of the Liberty Bridge, the steel building dead center over my forehead. I didn't know why I wanted it, but it seemed like the most important thing in the world at that moment. I felt a fury of competition, found my father in the audience and sang it straight to him, imagining that I was tiny, and the landscape on the crown was to scale and I was singing from the apex of the fountain at Point State Park. The part in my hair was a distant horizon, my huge feet like faraway constellations in an expansive space, every face in the audience a star, light years away from the gravity that ruled each heart. I imagined I was all alone in the universe, that the only way to be with the people I loved was to sing, each note forming a huge drift net that would snare everything and everyone I loved in the ropey coils of my voice.

I got a standing ovation, and for the first time in my life I knew what it meant to ache for someone who wasn't there, the terrible longing that defined grief.

We went to Tambellini's, my father's restaurant, for the victory celebration. I came in second—the first runner-up to another Exotic Other who scored better in the private interview with the judges.

The restaurant was filled to capacity with our huge extended family and friends of my father's who came up one by one to congratulate me. My father seemed baffled and confused, stunned; he hadn't said a word on the ride over. I asked him what was wrong; thinking his silence was disappointment, I apologized for not winning. But when he turned to me, I saw tears in his eyes.

"You're sorry?" he said. "No, don't ever be sorry. You are everything I never thought I would deserve. I am the luckiest man alive."

Except that he sat at the bar in the restaurant the whole night and hardly spoke. I was hurt, felt betrayed that he wasn't happier and swaggering around the way he did, for instance, when I came into the restaurant after school and he marched me back and forth through the dining room and bars, soliciting comments from people, beaming with pride when he told somebody that I was a straight A student.

I tried to forget him at the party, ignored his moody presence in the dark corner, and stuffed myself at the buffet table; it seemed I had never been hungrier in my life. My father had instructed his cooks to prepare all my favorite dishes. There was an obscene amount of food. Mrs. De Kamp and three of my best friends sat with me, but the whole night seemed cheerless and empty.

Later, in the car, I asked him if he was okay to drive; he'd had a lot to drink.

He gave a little sarcastic laugh and said, "What's the alternative, let you behind the wheel?"

His tone and expression made me feel as though I'd been slapped. "Why are you acting like this?"

"Like what?"

I shrugged. "Like I did something wrong. Are you upset because I didn't win?"

"Oh, God no. I was quite pleasantly surprised when you finished second."

I started to cry. It seemed his true opinion of me had come out at last, something I'd always sensed but never knew for sure until now.

"Oh, sweetheart," he said, "I'm sorry. I didn't mean that the way it sounded. Don't cry."

"You were the one who made me do this thing. I never wanted to be beautiful."

"I know, I know. Except that you are. You are beautiful."

I stared out into the cool September night, and pretended not to hear him.

He lit a cigarette. "I feel like my heart's been cracked open like a walnut, feel exactly like I did the night Anna died."

I turned to look at him. His hands shook as he flicked an ash into the tray. "You'll be bringing boys home soon. I'll have to stand there and smile when some young punk with ten dollars and tickets to a bargain matinee comes to claim you."

I didn't answer.

He started the car. "Now," he said. "Where can I take you?"

"Home, I guess."

"Home? Already? A winner in a beauty pageant wants to go home before eleven o'clock? I'm thinking the night should never end. Let an old man squire around his sweet pride."

I shrugged. "We could go downtown."

"Yes!" he said. "Downtown. We'll find something to do there." He stopped at the edge of the parking lot, looking either way. "Now: which way? Things are a little foggy. I'm a little drunk. Which way do I go? Point me in the right direction, Gina. Left or right?"

I pointed left, then closed my eyes and did not move or speak.

Where
Love
Leaves
Us

All around the fountain are tiny blue lights that cast shadows the color of twilight on the sculpted lovers in the center. The form of them changes with distance; up close their embrace is the tryst of all great passion: part despair, part delight, part unifying mystery. From my bedroom window or roof—where I sometimes sit and work on my photograph albums—the shape of the sculpture is not human at all, but something like a terrible, dark fish that heard a fatal note in the air and rose to it.

Bruno and I stand in the backyard the third evening I am home, and he holds me in mock imitation of them, laughing as he always does, though the figures are as familiar to him as I am. We were in love the summer we were both eighteen, but have since been able to stay lovers the way some people remain friends after the romance ends.

"So? Why are you here *this* time?" He backs me into the fountain so that my spine is pressed hard against the cement base. I pull him toward me and bend backwards so that my hair is immersed in the water. With his tongue, he traces the trail of water running down my neck.

"I've come home because, believe it or not, she asked me," I say, meaning my mother, C.D. Since being on my own, I have been home for six extended visits within seven years, the principal reasons being that I was between schools or jobs and not in love. I am a disgrace, according to C.D.—"twenty-five years old and still transitory"—but am not dissuaded from returning even after I came home last summer, after giving up my research assistantship, to find that I no longer had a bedroom. C.D. had redecorated it into a sewing room, complete with a large work table and a new French teal carpet the fallen needles in which I had to pick out of my soles every evening. She finally conceded and moved in the daybed from the guest room.

"I don't know what you want," she said last summer. I was sitting on the floor surrounded by romance novels—I indulge when I am on the rebound—and Butterick patterns. She leaned against the doorway in her nightgown, her cold-creamed face making her look like some sort of displaced mime. "They pay for your tuition, they give you a stipend. There are some people who would kill for that."

I said I didn't know what I wanted either, but what I *didn't* want or need was work that required me to assist in burning lab animals with a blow torch in order to experiment with skin grafting. My work is in genetics and I am opposed to vivisection for any and all purposes. She said, "You think you can get through life as a functional human being and not do certain things because they're contrary to your beliefs?" I said that I wasn't as concerned with getting through life functionally as I was with just getting through it.

Bruno puts his hand inside my shirt and leans into me. I turn my head and watch my hair floating in tendrils around my head, undulating gently like uncoiled roots. Bruno says something to me which I feel as a vibration in his chest against mine. He laughs and grabs my elbows, pulls me up so quickly that my hair drags my head back. The novelty buttons on his jacket jab my breasts. Mr. Ed (mouth open in mid-sentence) decorates one side of his collar, a day-glo green one with a black X that reads, "You are here," the other. I look at him, marveling as I always do at the physical beauty of this man—the way the last of the sun makes his skin and hair the color of autumn, the full mouth with its Botticelli lips, a sweet roof for the cleft in his chin which tempts my tongue. I succumb. I've had many men and have been in and out of love dozens, maybe hundreds, of times, but with Bruno I can never resist. The body has a memory of its own, remembering what has long been white ash in the mind.

"Lena love," he says, running the words together. For as long as I've known him he's called me this, his tongue gliding over the L's and held by the O's, looped and fastened. *Lenalove.*

"And it's good to see you," he says, squeezing the water out of my hair. "So why did the ice lady ask you back?"

Bruno has called C.D. this since we were in high school and she wouldn't let him in our house because he had a "reputation"—rumors of drug use (true) and petty theft (untrue). I think C.D. secretly fears Bruno because he is not *contained*; energy in all its forms is sexual and C.D. holds tight in her skin.

"Why else? She missed me."

He laughs and covers my ear lobe with his mouth. "Me, too."

"The ice lady has her reasons, I'm sure. Maybe it's just loneliness." Since my father died two years ago, C.D. has become less impatient with my visits home, but I do not deceive myself: if company is all she wanted, then she asked me only because my sisters declined. I do not mind. I am between semesters, but not schools or jobs, and this gives me the upper hand: sustained criticism of my lifestyle or attitude and I'm back in Chicago. Her life is threadbare, mine is full. I have love (Bruno here, a young biologist back in Illinois), which insulates, grounds me.

I turn to look at Bruno. He has moved to his motorcycle and is rolling a joint from the stash he keeps in the compartment under the seat. He glances at me then up at the house. C.D.'s form is silhouetted in the window, her body shaped in a half moon as she bends over the sewing machine. She spends hours there, though what she's working on she does not say or leave lying around for me to see.

"Do you think that's the only reason she asked you here?" Bruno says, lighting the cigarette.

"What? What reason?"

"Loneliness. Maybe she's into the reconciliation thing. Maybe she feels guilty."

"C.D. never feels guilty. And for what anyway?"

He shrugs. I take the joint from him and inhale, feel the smoke deep in my lungs. I straddle the seat behind him and hang on, waiting for the beautiful terror to come as it always does when I am high: the feeling that my skin will not hold me. "Drive."

He hands the joint over his shoulder to me and starts up the engine. I finish it off, the waves of the drug in my body numbing my limbs, making me feel buoyant and set to music. Bruno speeds down the highway, the emptiness of the road a void broken only by the headlight.

We stop at a clearing bordered by woods on three sides. Bruno spreads his jacket for me next to a fallen log, and I lie with my back against it, pulling him toward me so that I am anchored on both sides. I trace the line of his throat with my index finger. There is a certain tautness about the skin, as if the bones there push the words down before he can speak them. Bruno's words—always *chosen*—have a certain luster to them which stays with me and becomes my own, like pearls worn directly against the skin.

"What is it?"

He looks down at me. "What do you mean?"

I pull his jacket around my shoulders and lie on top of him so that he cannot avoid my eyes.

"Lena," he says, voice trailing off. *Love*, the crickets supply in answer. He reaches into the pocket of the jacket and takes out his cigarettes. I hold the lighter in front of his face, the glare causing his pupils to constrict, drawing expression into pinpoints. I toss the lighter aside and run my hand through his hair, pressing in on the scalp until his skull resists. "Tell me."

He gathers my wrists together in one hand. "What are you talking about?" He pries my fist open and kisses my palm. "Lena," he says, laughing. "You never were a good *substance abuser*. You always get paranoid. Remember the time when . . ." He draws me into reverie then to himself, our bodies melded as one shape. *Now now*—words I repeat for their sound.

C.D. has displaced or rearranged everything that is familiar: she has left me with a bed and a bureau which I've filled with what I've brought, but my father's walnut desk—which took three of us to move on my last visit home—is back downstairs in his study. Above her sewing machine the bookcase, save for two shelves, is filled with sewing paraphernalia. I make my way around scraps of fabric, using some as bookmarks: a wisp of Chantilly lace marks my place in *The Lives of a Cell*; a strip of blackwatch plaid in *The Origin of Species*. I keep what I own stacked beside me, reading every morning, exams and the search for a thesis topic looming. Symbiosis and its role in synchronicity comes to me as a potential topic as I finish the Lewis Thomas books and work my way through psychobiology and animal studies. I am fascinated by whales, their intelligence and communication through water vibrations that make rhythm a language. I read in one book that echolocation is to hearing what X-ray vision is to sight. And to a lesser extent, I am fascinated by the emotion of dolphins and seals. The mother seal mourns, *wails*, for the baby as she watches the hunters club it; the more beautiful the fur the more vigorous the blows. I saw on a Sunday morning nature show the mother seal's actual *tears* as she watched her baby being bludgeoned. She crawled toward the killers as they dragged it away. And then the stilling of her body, the motionlessness that comes with knowledge and surprise: where in this larger world, this land to which she doesn't belong, are the danger warnings the water and its rhythm provided? Danger creeps stealthily on the earth, cruelty leaves no tracks. But of course I'm anthropomorphizing, knowing even as I do that lesser mammals haven't the capacity for any pain that is not physical: the brain is underdeveloped, the cerebral cortex and frontal lobes crude.

The sun is not yet fully risen. I crawl out onto the roof with my photograph albums and loose pictures I want to affix. The air is cool, the light indefinite.

I spread out the photographs before me, grouping them according to dominant expression, postures, rather than chronological time. Most are of my father. He was a fine-looking man, and in each picture he is the subject, the center always, upstaging all others so that comparatively they are nothing more than negatives of themselves.

My father's expressions were never duplicated. In the hundreds of photographs I have of him, each one is subtly different—a testimony to his originality, genius: everything before and behind his eyes was forever new, though his three chief expressions were delight, despair, and surprise. The caption beneath one: "C.D., C.D., and Lena at eight." Both with the same initials (Carolyn Diana Healy, Charles Daniel Hayduke), the family joke is that my mother married him so she wouldn't have to change the monograms on her (L. L. Bean) sweaters or bath towels. In the photograph before me, my father (expression delight) holds me and leans against a rock wall at the beach. C.D. is herself an appendage. My sisters, two sitting at his feet and one behind him, are clusters of shadows. That was the summer we found out he had multiple sclerosis. In the photograph, all but my father hold the news on their faces.

C.D. and my sisters, unlike me, were afraid of the water, so my father and I together began and ended our days with the water and the sun. Arising just before dawn, we would stand at the shoreline and wait for the light to join the ocean with the sky at the horizon. ("Hear it *sizzle*; the morning, Lena, inhales.") We would wade in and he'd lift me when the water reached my neck, sleep still clinging to me like the early fog that hung over the water, my mouth tasting salt as we rose and fell with the rhythmic pulse of the waves. There was a church cemetery nearby, and from certain angles we could see the headstones that jutted from the grassy hillside. He'd look in that direction when the bells rang (whole notes resonating), tightening his grip on me as we waited for the last peal so he could ask, "How many dead people do you think are in that cemetery? (pause) They're all dead." Laughter cresting with the waves. And in the end, when the disease had weighted and paralyzed him, the water let us borrow time, the buoyancy making his body obey, the salt giving back what was rightfully his. The night I awoke to find him sitting by my bed, finger poised over the wheelchair's control panel, I did not need to ask. Into the night I took him, the air thick with the scent of fish, stopping at the water's edge where I helped him from his chair onto the sand. On his elbows he crawled, dragging his body as I pushed him from behind until we were fully immersed and I could steady him. "Nothing like a little reverse evolution," he said, laughing. I held him, bouncing gently, his body light as a child's, the delicate freckles on his scalp where his hair had parted making him seem somehow so vulnerable that I kissed him there. We felt ourselves being carried out, the current pulling us further away from shore, his wheelchair (seat of judgment) a tiny, forgotten anchor. "It wouldn't be so bad, would it, Love?" he said. "To be carried away, give yourself over to it, and just let the water wear you down." Three months later when I saw him in that hospital bed, body shrunken and tangled with tubes and machines that parodied the rhythms of life, this fine man who had lived, *loved*, and could heal others but not himself, I thought, Oh, I should have, should have let the water have us both where your last expression (and mine too) would have been one of delight and not surprise.

I gather up the photographs along with some maps and brochures that belonged to him. One is a pamphlet about the ruins of Pompeii— a place he always longed to visit but never did. Only when a thing is in ruins does it move toward importance, he said once. True, I know now: the instant a lover leaves is when he gains my respect. Love is born only out of wreckage.

I spend all afternoon on the roof waiting for Bruno, my body molten and languid in the hot sun, ideas flickering but not taking hold: eugenics, ancestral memory, and especially the possibility of learning in utero. I've read studies of geniuses made before birth simply by the pregnant woman reading aloud—particularly lyric poetry, since that is heard as much with the nerves as with the ears.

C.D. climbs out onto the roof as I look through the stacks of photographs and drink a peanut Coke (five shelled and roasted nuts in cola with ice, my father's "cure" for a hangover). Head to toe, she is dressed in a shade of blue formaldehyde would be if it could be projected visually: the palest hue of it, sick and cloying. She is wearing my shoes. She sits beside me and tosses aside the photographs without so much as a glance. "Well," she says, running her hand through her hair, the shell pink nails—my polish—catching the light as they sift beneath the dark (silken) strands.

"Yes?"

"Look, Lena . . ."

She watches as I stir the Coke with my finger, the skin of the peanuts sticking to the ice cubes. "Yes?"

"I've been dating someone. I thought you'd want to know."

"Yes. Well." I should have guessed this. Her self-possession lately, the air of languid fullness that could have come only from a lover. It is the precise reason I require so many men.

"I borrowed your shoes. I'd nothing to match this skirt." She smooths the pleats and picks at imaginary threads. "I made this one without a pattern," she says, lifting the skirt above her knees and examining the hem. The veins in her legs are visible through the damp, blue stockings and the nylon smells faintly of lilac. I look away and sift through the stack of photographs. Here's one that dates back to the early 1900s. It is of my grandfather as a little boy, wearing short pants and suspenders, sitting among a flock of geese, some in half-wing. I've kept it because his expression is replicated in my father: a look of fleeting delight with something dark just about to cross the features, the pale light in the eyes as though nothing precisely is *there.*

C.D.'s sandaled foot is in front of me and I slip a photograph of my father beneath her toes. She glances down at it. It's the one taken in London, at a medical conference. He is standing with a group of doctors, including a striking female physician with hair the color of firelight. C.D. draws in the corners of her pink-frosted mouth. "What are you trying to tell me?"

I picked this snapshot arbitrarily, but C.D. reads meaning into the smallest gestures. "If you have something to say, say it." She hands the photograph to me and takes off her shoes. "You think it's wrong of me to be seeing someone so soon?"

No. Two and a half years: time enough for both bodies to grow cold. I say, "Don't you think that's a remarkable picture of Daddy? It's my favorite of his bewilderment expressions. That's all I meant."

She nods, eyebrows arched. "He was a fine and courteous man."

We stare at the fountain—I always turn it on at midday—a fine spray of water misting our faces when the wind shifts. "What I wanted to tell you is that I'm going out for the day and to ask you if you would join us for dinner next week. Here. You're welcome to invite Bruno."

"You're kidding? Since when is Bruno welcome?"

"I've misjudged that boy. I think he cares deeply for you."

How do you know? I want to ask, but she stands to go. I lie back on the roof and close my eyes, trying to cool my over-heated brain.

A little later, I hear C.D.'s laughter, the sound of her (my) high heels clicking on the pavement, a car horn. I lean over the edge. That's not a car, that's a love story: a '57 Chevy convertible so well kept that it might be this year's newest model. C.D.'s friend looks good: blond, like Bruno, with nice forearms: muscular and well-proportioned. Bruno's forearms are the only part of him I don't love: they appear underslung, too short for his large hands. C.D.'s friend says something to her then bends her head toward him and kisses her hair.

By early evening she still has not returned. I spend hours in my room searching through my books for a possible thesis topic, but nothing is yielded. My prospectus is due in the department in ten days, which gives me about a week to come up with something, allowing time for the mail. I weigh the possibilities of microbiology, the genetic transmission of antibodies for the germs that live in the air. Or DNA and its role in speech, voice patterns: do we choose certain words, use certain inflections because we are genetically predisposed to them? And, by extension, what influence does voice tonality and modulation exert over others?

When I can stand the solitude and frustration no longer I call Bruno. A short time later he climbs in through the window as I am reading my father's *Physician's Desk Reference* and pamphlets on illicit drugs. Bruno straddles the chair backwards and grins idiotically, trying to make me look up and laugh.

"Marijuana in large quantities can cause impotence," I say, reading the side effects/contraindications column. "Be careful of the cannabis, Love."

He jumps up and dives onto the bed, scatters books to the floor. "I've got a little tucked away," he says, lifting my skirt and resting his head on my stomach. I pull him up by the hair. He smiles and rolls off the bed. It is twilight and the room darkens in golden shadows. Wreathed and muted in this light, objects seem indefinite, the dust motes in the beams falling across the carpet like cells that no longer hold. Bruno walks around the room picking up buttons and pattern pieces from C.D.'s sewing table.

"Let's go somewhere," I say.

"Well, Love, I'm not exactly dressed for fine dining," he says, holding a long pattern sheet against the front of his pants. "Perfect size twelve." I smile at him in the mirror. His hair is gold in the last of the sun.

"Bruno Bruno Bruno," I say, and think: what good is willpower when it's up against a boy with a headful of light?

"Yes, my little love biscuit," he says.

I rest my chin on his shoulder and look at our reflections. "You have the strangest place in my heart."

"Hey, now, you're not going Hallmark on me, are you?"

"No chance," I say.

He turns, his eyes filling with me as I undress and walk to where C.D. keeps a tin of mismatched buttons. I place a whole row of them down the front of me, my skin making them stick with its own sweaty heat.

"Lena," he whispers. With his tongue, he lifts the button I've placed in the valley of my throat then works his way downward, until I am entirely unfastened, ready to step out of my skin.

Later, we drive to the old barn at the edge of town where we first made love back in high school. We have used every part of it, including on top of the feed chute. It is in the middle of nowhere, surrounded by nothing except overgrown grass and shrubbery. There is no indication where the house might have—*must* have—stood. The mystery of it is what attracts us: what kind of people or force destroys the house and farm and leaves its repository? We speculate: the barn is magical, hundreds, thousands, of years old, the wood kept supple and durable by the love that still lingers within. Often, as we lay in the hayloft (light through the high window muted and oblique no matter what time of day), we've invented stories. Illicit affairs at midnight, two young lovers (Anna and Jacob), one of whom is married but unloved anywhere but here. They make love in front of the stable, the scent of hay and the darkness closing in on them, wondering themselves as the stillness is broken now and then by the stamp of a hoof against the hard earth, how many people before them have done the same thing? They might remark on how the animals link them to the future, the silent knowledge in velvet eyes looking on, passed on infinitely, threading through time. Here the story becomes irresolute: passion a given, the point of contention between us is always the fate of the lovers themselves. I would have the young woman, Anna, fall through the ice while skating on the lake. Though her body was used as a woman's should be, she would be driven by something unspeakable to risk moving to the center of the ice. Her weight does not hold. There is a crack beneath her and then the January water shocks against her, freezing forever what is finally clear (and fatal). Sometimes I have her young lover plagued by grief the rest of his days, his spirit murky and sluggish; often I have him assist in her death: it is he who chases her to the center and looks on as she falls through.

Bruno always imagines them to be outlaws hiding out, innocent except for the crime of love. His imagination always stops there, and he is given over to physicality: what the man feels inside the woman, the things she does to him—physical and spiritual—that make it as though they share just one skin.

The clandestine air, the solidity of the walls here, sometimes make me so restless that even passion is no good: Tell me you love me, I'll say to Bruno, but he just holds me and laughs, says, "Lena love, what is love anyway, but something only the body can speak?"

Bruno lights a joint and passes it to me. "I really shouldn't. It keeps me awake. C.D. will be at the sewing machine early, and I won't get any sleep."

"Where *is* the ice lady tonight?"

"Out for the day, night, who knows."

"Is she seeing someone? I've seen her around town with some guy."

"Why didn't you tell me before? Why didn't you ever say anything?"

He shrugs. "You never asked, exactly. What's the big deal, anyway? The ice lady found someone who'll risk the thaw. And as for you, my little furnace," he says, and moves on top of me.

The straw murmurs beneath us. I grab tightly to Bruno when I feel myself spiraling, weightless, my voice small.

"Lena Lena Lena." His body tightens against me.

The proof, Love, is what we're left with in the end—phrase that comes to me as I stare up through the high window. And now finding my own rhythm: "Say it. Say it."

"Lena *love*."

In my father's study I work on my thesis outline: ancestral memory and its role in genetic differentiation among human beings. If (I assert) DNA can subject the body to genetically rare mutations, why not a certain chemical retention in brain composition that allows memories to be inherited? Subheadings: the strongest emotions (love, fear, and jealousy) may, when incremental and repetitive, embed pathways in the brain that alter its genetic structure so that the same alteration, and thus the emotions and memories that go with it, are inherited from one generation to another.

It's a stretch—more in the realm of poetry than hard science—but it seems to be more applicable than my whale studies.

C.D. taps on the door then walks in, perfume a wave that announces her before I even look up.

"Well. How do I look?"

I glance at her. She is wearing a black satin skirt and a red jacket with sequins that catch and refract the light like little mirrors. Her lips are crimson.

"Very magnetic, C.D."

"You like it? I wasn't sure. I didn't want to appear too eager, if you know what I mean. I had to borrow another pair of your shoes."

I look around the side of the desk: the Saturday night black pumps with the sling-back straps. I smile, remembering. Ice lady, if those shoes could talk, they would direct you to the finest pair of wing-tips in Chicago where they stood, toe to toe, in a phone booth at midnight.

There is a softness to her face, a certain way the clothes move easily with her body—as if her lover himself had arranged the folds—that causes something to catch in my throat. She sits. Behind her a photograph of my father smiles over her shoulder. If you could see her now, I say to him silently, love would turn the air to salt, the body obeying once more.

"C.D., you look lovely."

She smiles and leans her elbows on the desk, "It's been a while, you know," she says, and runs her finger along my glass of peanut Coke.

I watch her hands. "Been a while for what?"

"Well, since I've given a dinner party." She sips the drink.

"Anyway, it's not a dinner party. It's just me and Bruno and your friend."

She nods, touches the cold glass to her forehead and cheeks. "Will you help me, though?"

"With?"

"With keeping conversation lively. You always did have more social skills than I."

She looks past me as I look at her, tugging at one of the pearl earrings that were a gift from my father. Her expression is flat, concealing intention.

———

Just enough light is left for us to see our reflections in the sliding glass doors in my father's study. C.D. and I watch, our images melded in the glass, as Bruno, holding a bouquet of flowers, pauses beside the fountain and speaks to C.D.'s guest (lover? boyfriend?). There is a space of pinkish light between their bodies, the upper half of the sculpture to the left of them like a dark, clutching arm.

"Oh, he is attractive, isn't he?"

I find her eyes in the glass, but can't tell who she's looking at. (One hand placed on each image, what would I feel? One like dry ice, the other a fragrant warmth: I grow cold, I fear.)

Bruno steps in first and across his face: surprise. "C.D., you look wonderful." He hands her the flowers and his expression softens into appreciation.

C.D. smiles back and turns, brings the stranger into our circle. "Bruno you've already met," she says, touching his shoulder. "And this is Lena."

He takes my hand and smiles. "Your mother tells me you're going to be a biologist."

He is of medium height, his body sinewy and compact in just the way I like best.

"Geneticist," I say.

The stranger, Richard, I learn over dessert, is a systems analyst and was introduced to C.D. by a friend of hers who was dating him at the time. He has that air of presence and purpose that most women find irresistible. He says little and is content, it seems, to watch C.D. as she speaks. He keeps her wine glass full, and smiles at me when she says something clever as if to say, Isn't she a rare thing? Who could capture her in words? And she: something that stepped out of a painting, skin white as ermine, jewels at her ears and the valley of her throat, and, as any woman in love will, attracting all eyes.

The candlelight flickers across the table, the flame held in the surface of the dark wood. I look at Bruno, cover his hand with mine, and think: there is no reason why we couldn't rediscover love. He glances from C.D. to me with a detached smile. Back then, at eighteen, love began as a hallucination we shared. We'd dropped acid in a corner stable of our barn. It was my second time, and he talked me through it, suggested images so that my fear would not cause nightcrawlers with the heads of bats to devour my flesh as I watched, as happened six months earlier.

"Now we are in a field of flowers," he said, and I saw them: crimson and purple peonies that grew bigger and fuller as I ran until they were as big as moons and flat as water lilies. The air caught in my lungs, thin and sharp, my legs stems that tore as I ran. Bruno (himself, yet *not* himself) caught me, held me, teeth flashing white, hands touching my breasts and thighs; something I could watch but not feel as I lay weighted in the straw, the night half-lidded as a turtle's eye. I said, "Am I *here*, or am I *there*?" Two of me, disjoined. "Everywhere and nowhere, Love." Solitude blanched the grass, a white pocket in which we spun, wrestled. His words, held within the white light, trickled into colors: Prisms of topaz and ruby resting on my eyelids, mouth. The air a canvas, I had but to breathe.

I turn to look at Bruno now, his face in profile. I want suddenly to put my lips to the delicate blue vein threaded over the bridge of his nose, to feel the pulse over the cool bone. He does not notice me. C.D., effusive and shimmering with all those sequins, draws him to herself. *Ice Lady, you had us all fooled.* She turns to look at me suddenly. Bruno and the stranger follow her gaze.

"You don't have much to say tonight, Lena."

I shrug. "Sorry," I say, but she holds my stare. "Is this a citation from the Conversation Police?"

Bruno and Richard laugh. I look down and pull toward myself all the candles on the table. (*Now*, Bruno, where am I?)

So, it'll be late: I have half a dozen prospective topics, some as detailed as sixteen pages, lying in piles on my father's desk. I can no longer work in my bedroom: C.D. is in a fever, patterns, fabric everywhere, working until midnight sometimes like some Penelope weaving, unweaving, afraid to finish. I grow restless, my body an inertia that even Bruno fails to move.

What do you own, Lena? Words in my head, voice an amalgamation of many.

I have given, have I not? My body suspended in countless nights, betraying me only once: the time I thought I had found it with a beautiful man from my biology class. Glances exchanged over microscopes for months, my hands forgetting what to do when I felt his eyes on me, though I'd done hundreds of dissections. And his surprised laughter when I cried after he split open the frog's belly and the purplish black eggs burst through the skin. And later, his breath on my neck, angry and shallow because that time I *couldn't.* "I don't know what bitches like you want," he said. Love—that time I was sure it was real—making the body tighten in fear of losing what only it can give.

But now, Lena, what do you own?

Nothing. But emptiness is a kind of phenomenon.

And love?

Something I whipped into white heat with words.

Symbiosis and synchronicity; eugenics; ancestral memory; none of these will do. I write a note instead to my thesis advisor, making excuses for what I don't yet have.

C.D. knocks on the door then walks in. She is holding a hair-permanent kit and tiny pink and gray curlers. "I know you're busy, Lena, but Richard is taking me out tonight and look," she says, holding out a strand of limp hair. "Would you mind?"

I shake my head no, and we go outside—the odor of the solution lingers in the house for days otherwise. She opens a folding chair then sits, handing me curlers and comb. It has been years since I've worked on her hair. There are silver strands beginning at the crown, but otherwise it is as dark as mine (and as soft). I work the comb through it, neither of us speaking. My father's funeral was the last time we had any sort of physical contact. A slight shock goes through me as I stare down the part in her hair.

"So," she says after a few minutes. "What did you think of Richard?"

I thread a strand of hair through a curler and roll it as close to her scalp as I can get it, tightening, tightening. "I could see the attraction there."

"I think I'm in love with him. I haven't felt this way in twenty years. That's a little too tight. I don't want kinkiness," she says, touching the one I've just rolled.

"Twenty years?" The teeth of the comb glint silver in the sun.

"Well, you know what I mean. I'd just forgotten how it *feels*."

"How does it feel?" I rest my hand on her head. I can feel the vibrations of her speech, then her laughter, through her skull.

"Oh, Lena, *you*. You who've had so many boyfriends."

I finish the rows at the back of her head, alternating pink rollers with gray so the curls will vary in size.

"Easy, easy. My scalp is sensitive." She straightens her back and reaches around to where my hand is.

"So how *does* it feel, C.D.?"

She takes the question rhetorically and laughs again. "Something about younger men . . . they're always so *ready*. I don't mean physically. I mean a certain generosity of spirit. Richard is only three years younger than I am, but it makes a difference." She turns her head slightly, catches my eye out of the corner of hers. "You know, over the years I've watched you bring a parade of young men through the house . . . well, envy can take the form of disapproval, can't it? And Bruno . . ."

"What about Bruno?" I pick up the bottle of permanent solution and pull off the tab at the nozzle.

C.D., smelling the odor of the apple pectin, turns around to look. "Not too much of that. It makes the curls set in stiff."

"What about Bruno?"

"Oh, well, you two. He's a fine young man, Lena. I've just recently begun to see that."

I squeeze the bottle in even rows, carefully soaking each curl.

"I thought maybe the four of us could go on a picnic or something this weekend. Do you have much work to do?"

"Why all of a sudden are you so interested in Bruno?"

She turns abruptly. "How much of that are you using?" she says, looking at the bottle in my hand.

"Will you just turn around and relax, please? I've done this a hundred times. I know what I'm doing. You're making *me* nervous, for Chrissake."

"Well. You don't have to curse."

"I asked you why you're so interested in Bruno."

"Well, because you and Bruno keep me young. Young ideas."

I empty the rest of the bottle on her head and open the second. "What does that mean exactly?"

"What I mean is, I've *learned* from you, Lena."

I stare down at the rows of curls twisted around the rollers like tiny, precise waves. "You used me."

"What? What did you say?"

My vision blurs. "I said you *used* me. Is that why you asked me home? That's it, isn't it? Of course. You figure you're a little rusty in the romance department so you'd ask the slut home and observe. She's fucked hundreds. *She* must know what men want."

"Lena!"

"But you're no better. All those times, all I ever wanted was someone to love me. I thought if I could find at least one person to love me then I wouldn't just be some hunk of ice spinning through space. God knows I had no example from you. You stopped loving him the moment he got sick. And *now*, now you think you can just imitate the way I dress, my mannerisms, and know what I know?"

"My God, I didn't mean . . . didn't know."

My fingers tighten around the middle of the bottle. Curls at the crown glisten, gullies between them filling and overflowing toward her temples.

She jumps up, making little sounds in her throat. "It's in my eyes! It's running into my eyes." She closes them tightly, acid forming a gummy seal. I take her arm and lead her to the fountain.

"It's burning. I can feel it burning right through the tissue."

I push her head into the water. "Open your eyes. Open them. The water will flush out the poison."

"You did that on purpose," she says, gasping. "You poured that into my eyes deliberately." She holds the towel to her face and sinks to the earth, cheek pressed against the cement base of the fountain. She looks up at me, the weariness of age now on her face. Her eyes are red slits, already swollen and heavy as a blossom. *Receive now the dispensation of my knowledge.*

I walk a straight path to the house feeling light as an ash in the wind.

Upstairs in the hallway, where it has again become an ordinary table, is the sewing machine, leaves folded over, a flat surface out of which the vase of Bruno's flowers rise. My bedroom door is closed. I nudge it open with my foot.

Words rush up and die in my throat. C.D. has clothed the room—bedspread, curtains, vanity skirt—in matching dark blue fabric with a tiny beige print. The bed meets the window, the print of the spread rising, cresting at the pillows and splitting in two where the curtains are parted with eyelet, the pink light between opening out to the sky. My legs will not hold. I sink to the floor, feeling each bone in my spine against the door frame, and am freezing cold suddenly despite the midsummer heat.

What is love but something only the body can speak?

Out of the corner of my eye I see her form. I turn. Her hair is in waves now, released from the curlers. She sits in the corner opposite me, the surprise still on her face and now mirrored in my own.

"I just wanted to give you something. I just wanted you to feel welcome again. That's all."

We watch as the last of the twilight sinks behind the mountains. Shapes disappear in the dark. The night is broken by the steady rhythm of her hair dripping onto the carpet: the sound of a thaw. The sound of a seal's tears after the hunters have come.

*Other Iowa Short
Fiction Award and
John Simmons
Short Fiction Award
Winners*

1992
My Body to You, Elizabeth Searle
Judge: James Salter

1992
Imaginary Men, Enid Shomer
Judge: James Salter

1991
The Ant Generator,
Elizabeth Harris
Judge: Marilynne Robinson

1991
Traps, Sondra Spatt Olsen
Judge: Marilynne Robinson

1990
A Hole in the Language,
Marly Swick
Judge: Jayne Anne Phillips

1989
Lent: The Slow Fast,
Starkey Flythe, Jr.
Judge: Gail Godwin

1989
Line of Fall, Miles Wilson
Judge: Gail Godwin

1988
The Long White,
Sharon Dilworth
Judge: Robert Stone

1988
The Venus Tree, Michael Pritchett
Judge: Robert Stone

1987
Fruit of the Month, Abby Frucht
Judge: Alison Lurie

1987
Star Game, Lucia Nevai
Judge: Alison Lurie

1986
Eminent Domain, Dan O'Brien
Judge: Iowa Writers' Workshop

1986
Resurrectionists, Russell Working
Judge: Tobias Wolff

1985
Dancing in the Movies,
Robert Boswell
Judge: Tim O'Brien

1984
Old Wives' Tales, Susan M. Dodd
Judge: Frederick Busch

1983
Heart Failure, Ivy Goodman
Judge: Alice Adams

1982
Shiny Objects, Dianne Benedict
Judge: Raymond Carver

1981
The Phototropic Woman,
Annabel Thomas
Judge: Doris Grumbach

1980
Impossible Appetites,
James Fetler
Judge: Francine du Plessix Gray

1979
Fly Away Home, Mary Hedin
Judge: John Gardner

1978
A Nest of Hooks, Lon Otto
Judge: Stanley Elkin

1977
The Women in the Mirror,
Pat Carr
Judge: Leonard Michaels

1976
The Black Velvet Girl,
C. E. Poverman
Judge: Donald Barthelme

1975
*Harry Belten and the
Mendelssohn Violin Concerto*,
Barry Targan
Judge: George P. Garrett

1974
*After the First Death There Is No
Other*, Natalie L. M. Petesch
Judge: William H. Gass

1973
The Itinerary of Beggars,
H. E. Francis
Judge: John Hawkes

1972
The Burning and Other Stories,
Jack Cady
Judge: Joyce Carol Oates

1971
*Old Morals, Small Continents,
Darker Times*, Philip F. O'Connor
Judge: George P. Elliott

1970
The Beach Umbrella,
Cyrus Colter
Judges: Vance Bourjaily and
Kurt Vonnegut, Jr.